Anandibai
and Other Stories

The sculpture reproduced on the endpaper depicts a scene where three soothsayers are interpreting to King Suddhodana the dream of Queen Maya, mother of Lord Buddha. Below them is seated a scribe recording the interpretation. This is perhaps the earliest available pictorial record of the art of writing in India.

From Nagarjunakonda, 2nd century A.D.

Courtesy: National Museum, New Delhi.

SAHITYA AKADEMI AWARD WINNING BENGALI STORIES.

ANANDIBAI
AND OTHER STORIES

Parashuram

Translated by
Swapna Dutta

Sahitya Akademi

Anandibai and Other Stories – English translation by Swapna Dutta, of 'Parashuram's Bengali short stories entitled, *Anandibai Ityadi Galpa*. Sahitya Akademi, New Delhi 1992.

©English translation : Sahitya Akademi
First Published : 1992

Sahitya Akademi

Rabindra Bhavan, 35 Ferozshah Road,
New Delhi - 110 001
Sales: 'Swati', Mandir Marg, New Delhi - 110 001
'Jeevan Tara Building', 4th Floor,
23A/44 X, Diamond Harbour Road, Calcutta - 700 053
ADA, Rangamandira, 109 J.C.Road, Bangalore - 560 002
172, Mumbai Marathi Grantha Sangrahaalaya Marg,
Dadar, Bombay - 400 014
Guna Buildings 2nd floor,
304-305, Anna Salai, Teynampet, Madras - 600 018

ISBN 81-7201-263-2

Rs. 40/-

Published by the Sahitya Akademi, New Delhi, and printed at Gee Bee Graphics, 40/3, M.S. Naidu Street, Madras - 600 021.

Contents

Foreword	 7
Anandibai	 12
The Elixir of Exhilaration	 24
The Creation of Bateswar	 34
The Celestial Strip-tease	 47
Scholar Dambaru	 54
The Two Lions	 65
The Sheep-makers	 76
The Reincarnation of Kashinath	 84
The Heavenly Slippers	... 100
The Exchange	... 110
Queen Buffalo	... 124
The Letter Race	... 136
The Truth Seeker	... 145
The Transformation	... 156

Contents

Foreword

Introduction

The Dawn of Civilisation

The City they Murdered

The Unequal Conquerors

Semitic Triumph

The Twin Lands

The Sea-traders

The Coming of the Railways

The Heavenly Kingdom

Carthage

Greek Patriots

The Barbarians

The Holy Cities

The Reformation

FOREWORD

Raj Shekhar Bose, eminent scholar, scientist and writer who simplified and shortened the Ramayana and the Mahabharata from the original Sanskrit into Bengali for the common reader and compiled the 'Chalantika' - a popular Bengali dictionary, copiously used by students, scholars and authors alike - chose 'Parashuram' as his pen-name when writing stories of humour. The axe of the mythological Parashuram symbolised power. The weapon dear to our Parashuram - the pen - symbolised laughter. He is one of the greatest Indian humourists of the present century.

Parashuram's place in literature is somewhat unique. Being a scientist by profession, he did not wield his pen for the sake of livelihood. Indifferent to publicity of any kind, he never felt the temptation to churn out stories by the dozen. Nevertheless he shot to fame, making a secure and permanent place in the hearts of his readers, with his very first story - 'Sri Sri Siddheswari Ltd', written at the mature age of forty-two. As is obvious from his stories, Parashuram wrote for the sheer love of creation, unaffected and untouched by any other consideration. His stories - though not very many in number - are gems, sparkling with wit and satire, laughter and light-hearted fun.

Every writer is influenced by the age he lives in. The social set-up, the norms, ideals, ideas and lifestyle of the period coupled with the particular kind of education received by him - all play a role in moulding him as a writer. That is why, it is important to know the basic facts about an author's life and the age he belongs to. Unfortunately Parashuram was not interested in writing about himself. He has left us no autobiography. And for some inexplicable reason (or is it coincidence?), no biographer has come forward with a good, comprehensive life-story of Parashuram. But luckily for us, several well known men of letters - Pramatha Nath Bisi, Kalidas Ray, Anurupa Devi, Sashi Shekhar Basu, Charu Chandra Bhattacharya, amongst others - have written about their personal relationship and impressions of the author. Taken together, specially Pramatha Nath Bisi's scholarly epistle on Parashuram, they provide us with quite a clear picture of the man - his life and times.

Born on 16th March, 1880, Parashuram was named 'Raj Shekhar' after the Rajah of Darbhanga, who was well known to his father Chandra Shekhar. Little Raj Shekhar showed a marked curiosity about things - which later developed into a scientific temper - right from his childhood. He wanted to know how things worked. The moment his parents gave him a toy - be it a railway engine or a tin-whistle he immediately broke it apart, trying to see what made it work. He had his early schooling in Munghyr and went on to complete his 'First Arts' from Patna College. He came to Calcutta after that and graduated from the Presidency College with physics and chemistry as his main subjects. He took his master's degree in chemistry, standing first in the university. Then he decided to go in for law and took his B.L. degree. But just three days in the court covinced him that becoming a lawyer was not his cup of tea! He was cut out for something totally different. His close contact with two of the country's leading scientists, Sir J.C Bose and Sir P.C. Ray, soon made him realise that his real forte lay in scientific research. He joined the Bengal Chemicals as a chemist in 1903 and was made the manager of the entire concern in a year's time. He remained with the Bengal Chemicals until his retirement in 1932. It is important to know this scientific background of Parashuram. His knowledge of science and law influenced his style of writing to a great extent - making his language simple, logical, lucid, brief, concise, direct and to-the-point. It has been said that brevity is the soul of wit. Parashuram's stories are living examples of this statement. Though they bubble ever with fun and merriment, Parashuram never wastes words. Every word he writes is significant.

The Boses had their ancestral home at 14 Parsi Bagan, Calcutta. Parashuram and his three brothers were all fond of socialising. Their home was the merry and jovial meeting place of countless scientists and men of letters, doctors and professors, artists and scholars, psychologists and historians, writers and journalists of repute. They thronged every evening, specially on Sundays and holidays. Science and politics, classics and poetry, law and literature - everything was discussed over cups of tea, usually made by artist Jatindra Nath Sen, who illustrated many of Parashuram's books. It was virtually a club. Parashuram named it the 'Utkendra Samiti'. Regular members included stalwarts like Jadu Nath Sarkar, Prabhat Muhkopadhyay, Sarat Chandra Chattopadhyay, Suniti Chattopadhyay, amongst others. These meets left their mark in the stories of Parashuram. They cover a vast range of themes and characters - from scientists to characters from the Puranas - and every word spoken by his creations ring true. In fact, the club at Parsi

Bagan has been immortalised in several of his stories where he calls the place '14 Habsi Bagan'.

Pramatha Nath Bisi has compared humour to the rainbow, each kind of humour symbolising a particular colour of the spectrum. On the one hand, humour can consist of pure comedy based on sheer light-hearted fun, totally free from malice or criticism. This has been compared to red, one end of the vibgyor. Humour can also consist of biting satire, a whip that lashes out towards the flaws and drawbacks of our society and yet make us laugh at it. This has been compared to violet, the other end of the spectrum. The colours in between contain a mixture of these two emotions in varying degrees.

Parashuram's humour contains all the colours of the rainbow, though most of his stories tend to lean towards satire. They appeal to our intellect as well as our heart. That is why we cannot forget them even after we have laughed over them. They make us think. This is true of every single story. Whether it is about an attractive, yet, hardened rogue like Jatadhar Bakshi or a born fool like Dambaru Pandit, an insufferable egoist like Bateswar Sikdar or a smart operator like Kapot Guha, a fond and foolish husband like Seth Trikram Das or an over-cautious pair like Sunanda and Sukanto!

What gives Parashuram's humour its special and distinctive tang is his ability to combine light - hearted fun with biting satire in such a deft and neat manner that his stories evoke laughter and awareness without hurting anyone. His blows are not aimed at any particular individual or community. He lays bare the sham and hypocrisy of society and human nature without bias or partiality of any kind. His targets are norms, ideologies and professions which are turned into ludicrous, ridiculous and shameless fiascos by people who are selfish, unprincipled and unscrupulous. The cap could fit just anybody in the society! Every single character is familiar. That is why the reader is able to laugh at the victim, realising at the same time what he ought to have done.

Reading Parashuram is a delightful experience. Translating his stories is, by no means, an easy task. Even the most successful translator is bound to feel dissatisfied at his/her ability to convey the irresistible charm of the original in an alien tongue. At best it can be a tame black-and-white version of a painting done in glowing technicolour. But it is better than nothing. Parashuram is one of these authors who deserve to be read by all, even when the translation happens to be a poor substitute for the original.

Kanpur   **Swapna Dutta**
1st January 1992

Anandibai

Trikram Das Karori - the owner of several business concerns - sat signing cheques in the special chamber of his Delhi office when his bearer brought in a card bearing the name of Mr. Zulfikar Khan. "Ask him to wait a minute," said Trikram Das, glancing at the card.

In a short while the clerk left the room carrying a sheaf of signed cheques. Trikram rang the bell and handed the card to his bearer. "Show him in," he said.

"Adaab arz, Sethji," said Zulfikar Khan stepping into the room. "I'm from the Intelligence Branch."

"Anything wrong?" asked Trikram in an anxious voice. "Don't tell me some new trouble has cropped up regarding my income-tax!"

"Well, I don't know about that. But there *is* a serious charge levelled against you from my department."

"Indeed! What am I supposed to have done?"

"You've taken three wives."

Trikram guffawed loudly. "Is that all? And what if I have? I am a Hindu so I can get married as many times as I want to - unlike you people, who have to restrict yourselves to just four wives. "

Khan waved his hand and said, "Gracious, Sethji," you're quite impossible! All you know is money - making! Don't you know anything about what has been happening in the country? A law has already been passed which proclaims that no Hindu, Buddhist, Jain or Sikh may take more than one wife at a time.

"You don't say so!" cried Sethji. "I've been so busy with a thousand and one things that it hasn't always been possible for me to keep track of current affairs. Of Course I always make it a point to find out what new taxes have been introduced and whether fresh licenses are required and all that sort of thing. In any case, I can't quite believe what you're telling me. My own uncle - Harchandji - has been living merrily with both his wives. I'm sure no charges have been levelled against him!"

"My dear Sethji, your uncle already had two wives before the new law came into existence. So naturally it is not going to affect him! But you have married three times quite recently - for which you're going to face the music! Ten years of rigorous imprisonment and most probably a heavy fine as well."

Sethji, suitably impressed, turned on a panic-stricken voice. "I'm in a real mess, it seems! Tell me, what on earth am I to do?"

"Well Sethji, you're a well-known personality. And a well-to-do one. We've no wish to harass you unnecessarily, so we'll grant you a month's time to sort things out."

"What's it going to cost me?"

"Well, you have to keep just one wife and get rid of the other two. I've no idea what compensation they're going to demand of you. You'd better take expert legal opinion for that. As for the rest, that is strictly between you and me! We can discuss it once this tangle has been straightened."

Trikram Das struck his forehead in despair. "Lord Rama save me! I don't see how I'm to manage it. I've married one of them the traditional way, another according to Arya Samaj rituals and I've had a Civil Court marriage with the third. How can I possibly get rid of them now?"

"Don't worry. Sethji, you don't lack money, after all! Spend a lakh or two and get it all settled up. You've only got to present large sums of money to any two of your wives and get them to give it to you in writing that they are merely your adored mistresses and *Not* your legally-wedded wives! That's all! Once they do it, we shall suppress the whole affair. But you can't afford to waste *Any* time! Get in touch with a good lawyer this very instant. So long for now! See you again next week!"

Trikram Das, having crossed fifty quite some time ago, had a rather unusual marital history. His first wife - the only one till then - had died a couple of years ago, leaving a number of children behind. He had married Anandibai a few months later and had followed it up with two more quick marriages. Needless to say, he had not thought it necessary to inform his friends and relatives about his last two wives. And that included Anandibai.

Anandibai was the only child of Harjeevan Lal, the retired dewan of Khajauli Estate. He was the owner of a large property. When he passed away, one of his distant cousins tried to take on the guardianship of Anandi, with the intention of grabbing it himself. But Trikram managed to put his oar in, get hold of the business himself and get it all under his thumb by marrying Anandi. Anandi, whose age was somewhere around twenty-five, was somewhat homely to look at. She was also a garrulous sort and immensely proud of her high family connections.

Trikram Das had his head-office - which was his real business centre in Delhi. He also had fairly large branch offices in Bombay and Calcutta. He went to inspect the latter two personally thrice or four times a year. He had been to visit his Bombay branch office soon after he got married to Anandi. Kishan Ram Khobani, the manager, invited him to his place. Kishan Ram belonged to Sindh originally but he had migrated to Delhi soon after the partition. He had joined Trikram's business and had soon been transferred to Bombay as the Branch Manager. He had an artistic temperament which was fairly obvious from his well furnished flat. He introduced his boss to his wife and sister-in-law.

Now, Sethji was an old fashioned man, never having set his eyes on truly 'modern' women. He was absolutely enchanted with Rajhansi Jhalkani, Kishan Ram's sister-in-law. How fair she was! And so exquisitely dressed! Her light blue salwar, the matching deep blue Kurta and the gleaming green dupatta, with sequins sparkling all over it, made his heart turn right over! And how sweetly she requested him to taste the various dishes! There was not a trace of reserve or shyness about her!

Once they finished their meal Sethji, called Ram Kishan aside and asked him all about Rajhansi. He soon learnt that she had no parents and her only brother who ran a roaring business in Singapore took no notice of her whatsoever. That is why Kishan had been compelled to offer her a home. Rajhansi was rather good at acting, had a melodious voice and was determined to become a film-star. But both Kishan and his wife were dead against the idea.

Sethji made up his mind on the spot. "I want to marry Rajhansi so you'd better arrange it," he said. "I shall give her every comfort. And of course I must have a house in Bombay so you'd better buy one fast. Rajhansi can stay there. I too shall live in Bombay most of the time and enlarge my business here."

Sethji did not think it necessary to bring Anandi into the picture so he did not mention her at all. Ram Kishan had heard that his boss's wife had died very recently, so he gladly agreed to the match. Rajhansi agreed too and did not seem to mind his age. They were married according to Arya Samaj rites. The house was bought and Rajhansi installed in her new home.

After a few days Trikram Das went to inspect his Calcutta branch office. Paritosh Hor Choudhury, the manager, was a most efficient man and lived in Alipore in real English style. He invited his boss to dinner, escorting him to his bungalow personally - and introduced him to his wife and sister. Sethji was swept off his feet at the sight of Miss Balaka Hor Choudhury. True, she wasn't as beautiful as Rajhansi but how elegantly she wore the sari! And conducted herself with such style! Why, she could speak English like an English woman! Although her Hindi was a different cup of tea, how very sweet her mistakes sounded! Sethji lost his heart to Balaka - lock stock and barrel! Paritosh informed him that Balaka was an M.A., an expert dancer and musician and considered to be a paragon and a non-pareil on the Calcutta scene. And of course the film - makers were constantly making a bee-line for her. But Paritosh was dead against her joining films.

Sethji, unable to hold back his emotions any longer blurted out, "Miss Balaka, I shall marry you."

"Very well", said Balaka, smiling at him. "But I'm afraid I cannot stand the Delhi heat. Nor can I possibly get accustomed to your diet of dal, roti, bhaji and dahi-vada."

"Goodness! Why on earth need you go to Delhi?" cried Sethji. "I am going to buy a house right here in Alipore so that you can live near your brother. I'm very keen to enlarge my Calcutta business so I intend to live here for not less than eight to nine months a year. And there's absolutely no need for you to eat dal and roti. You are welcome to your fish and rice! I wouldn't have minded tasting fish myself if it didn't stink so badly!"

"Well I shall cook fish specially for you, using strong scented rose-water, so that it tastes just like kalakand sandesh", said Balaka. She had already heard from her brother that his boss was a widower. So she agreed to marry him at once. They had a civil marriage in three week's time. Trikram Das shunted between Delhi, Calcutta and Bombay, making a go of all three marriages and having a jolly good time into the bargain. That is, until Zulfikar Khan shattered his peace of mind one fine morning, by informing him about the tiresome new law about polygamy.

Khajan Chand, B.A., L.L.B., was a devoted and trusted friend of Trikram Das. The latter always depended on him for sorting out his income-tax hassles every year. He made up his mind to see Khajan Chand that very evening and tell him about the mess he was in. Khajan Chand rebuked him in no uncertain terms. "You've acted like a foolish kid," he told Sethji, "what a pity you never bothered to tell me about these two dames in Bombay and Calcutta before promising to marry either of them!"

"Forgive me, my friend," said Sethji in a penitent voice, folding both his hands, "I couldn't quite bring myself to tell you that I was hankering after two more females at my age - in spite of having a wife! Anyway, tell me how I can get out of this tangle."

Khajan Chand thought for a while and said, "You'd better not say anything to Anandi. It will upset her too much and she's likely to cry her eyes out. Tell the other two about the actual state of affairs. They are both modern girls, which means, they're likely to have some self-respect. Once they find out about your goings-on with three wives, they are sure to be hopping mad and probably refuse to see your face ever again! Which, of course, will solely be to your advantage. It will just mean a heavy compensation for the two females and possibly some hush-money for the two managers. You might have to dish out a couple of lakhs but you won't mind that."

Unfortunately this piece of advice did not appeal to Trikram Das at all. "My dear brother," he said to Khajan, "you haven't been able to comprehend the situation at all! I am very keen to enlarge my business. Which means I must socialise with important people. Supposing I were to throw a party for ministers and high-up government officials, which of my wives should I choose to play hostess? Anandi? Heaven forbid! The two who are really cut out for the job are Rajhansi and Balaka. If I must get rid of any of my wives, it certainly ought to be Anandi. Of course, it is going to break my heart because it also means losing a lot of property, but I'm quite prepared to do it. The real problem is to decide between Rajhansi and Balaka. I just can't make up my mind as to whom I should retain although I must confess to being somewhat partial to the Calcuttan. But in case I can't get her to agree, I'd settle for the Bombayite. Don't worry about money, though. I can very well spend up to ten or fifteen lakhs."

Khajan Chand tried his level best to convince Sethji that Anandi, by virtue of being his traditionally married wife, had the highest claim on him. Trying to get rid of her would mean having to face a great deal of hanky-panky, not to mention losing all the property inherited through her! The loss, he added, would be very considerable and he would end up right under the thumb of Anandi's villainous uncle. But Trikram just refused to see reason! Eventually Khajan was compelled to agree to his wishes and said that he would see how best he could handle the whole affair. "You'd better make a clean breast of everything to all three of them," he told Trikram, "I'll decide about my future line of action after I see how they react to your confessions."

Trikram did not waste any time. He flew to Bombay and landed up at Rajhansi's house the moment he reached there. Rajhansi was in the drawing room, chatting with a well-dressed young man. Taken aback by Sethji's sudden arrival, she cried, "Goodness! Sethji, to what do I owe this most unexpected visit? Why on earth didn't you let me know that you were coming? Anyway, I don't suppose you've met this gentleman before. He is Mr. Jhoot Kamal Matkani, a distant cousin of mine. He's a real whiz at keeping accounts so you'd better get rid of your old accountant at the Bombay office - it's time he retired, anyway - and give the job to Mr. Matkani instead."

"I'll give it a thought," said Trikram. "In the meantime, I must discuss something important with you."

Jhoot Kamal made a hasty exit. Sethji then disclosed his secret with a trembling heart. But Rajhansi's reaction to the news was totally unexpected. She burst into peals of laughter and said, "Bravo, Sethji! I never imagined you were such a colourful personality! I don't care in the least if you have two more wives - its a trivial thing, after all - so long as people at large don't get to know about it! Incidentally, I think you should get this house registered in my name as soon as possible. The muncipality has been harrassing me a great deal."

"Very well, I shall see to it," said Sethji, not quite knowing how to react. "But I'm afraid I can't stay back now. I must leave for Calcutta on urgent business this very instant."

On reaching Calcutta Trikram rushed to Balaka's house at Alipore. A handsome young man was playing the piano in the drawing room while Balaka swayed to his music. She was astounded to see Trikram. "Why this sudden visit, Sethji?" she cried. "I don't think you have met this gentleman before. He is Mr. Lotan Kumar Bhar, a distant cousin of mine. He is a fab dancer! I've been learning the pigeon-dance from him. Would you like me to do it for you right now?"

"I'm hard pressed for time at the moment," said Sethji, "besides, I've an urgent matter to discuss with you."

Once Lotan Kumar left them alone, Trikram told Balaka about his three marriages, his heart a-flutter with anxiety. But Balaka merely put a finger on her cheek and exclaimed, "Indeed? Well Sethji, you are a real deep one! A naughty playboy! But don't look so upset, for goodness sake! What on earth does it matter if you have three wives? Don't worry about me. I'm not the jealous sort, anyway. But please don't go around blabbing about it to every one! Oh that reminds me, I simply must have a new car, you know. The old Austin is no use and has to be repaired if one so much as moves it! You'd better give me a cheque for twenty thousand. It's quite impossible to get a decent car for less."

Trikram said, "Very well, I'll arrange it but I must

get going now. I've got to reach Delhi by evening"

Trikram made a bee-line for Khajan Chand the moment he reached the capital and told him all that had happened. Then he went to his own house, taking Khajan along with him. Asking him to wait in his drawing room, Trikram called Anandi to the bedroom. "What's up?" asked Anandi in surprise. "You've been missing for the last three days and you look positively haggard! Are you in some kind of a jam with the government again?

Trikram hung down his head and stammered out his confession. Anandi listened to him in dumb astonishment. Finally, she placed her hands on her hips, rolled her eyes and screamed, "What did you say, you blighter?"

Trikram, taken aback by her tone, hastily muttered, "Calm down, Anandi, calm down! All will be well."

However rich Bengali literature might be, it cannot possibly hold a candle to Hindi when it comes to choice abuses! Anandi flung her arms about and literally danced about in rage, a stream of abuses gushing out of her mouth like water from a hose-pipe, strong and soul shattering, all of them. Needless to say, not all of them were fit for a gentleman's ears and certainly not fit to be uttered by a lady! But Anandi was lost to all sense of propriety. Seeing her rising temper Trikram folded his hands and said in a feeble voice, "Forgive me, Anandi. All will be well again, you'll see."

Anandi let out a regular snarl, "Shut up, you cur-of-the-street, you mole-of-the-drains!" Then she jumped up like a tigress and scratched Trikram on both cheeks. Then she stepped back, took off the ten thick bangles from her left wrist and threw them straight at her husband. The bangles jingled as they struck him on the forhead. Trikram screamed when he saw the blood gushing out and fell on the ground with a thud. Anandi screamed even louder as she dashed off into the puja-room. Once there, she threw herself on the floor and sobbed her heart out. A regular pandemonium followed. The relatives rushed to console Anandi while Khajan rushed off to fetch a doctor for Trikram.

A whole week passed by. Trikram, feeling immensely better, sat smoking his hookah on the first-floor balcony. His head was still bandaged and there were several sticking plasters on both his cheeks. Khajan Chand having dropped in to enquire about his health, asked him how he felt now.

"Much better," said Trikram and added, "Look here, I don't wish to have anything more to do with either Rajhansi or Balaka. So you'd better go to Bombay and Calcutta pronto and settle up things with them. I'm quite willing to cough up whatever they ask for. The wretched Calcuttan and the Bombayite are just after my money and don't care a damn about me. But Anandi wants me for myself alone! Can't you smell something delicious? It's Anandi cooking khichri for me with her own hands. And just look at this woollen muffler which she has knitted for me."

"That's good news indeed!" said Khajan Chand. "Don't worry, Sethji. I'll manage everything else. In the meantime, take Anandi to visit Mathura, Vrindavan and Dwaraka. It is bound to put her into a sweet temper."

Anandi's care soon rendered Trikram perfectly fit. Khajan Chand also succeeded in settling matters to every one's satisfaction. Rajhansi and Balaka were content while Zulfikar Khan received a handsome present for "tasting paan". Anandi procured a "taming medallion" from Sri Jyotish Chandra Jyotish Arnaba, the famous astrologer from Calcutta, and hung it round her husband's neck. The medallion has been quite magically effective because now Trikram tells all his friends that except for Anandibai, all other females are outright banshees. *

---

* The plot is based on an English story. I do not remember the title.
— author

The Elixir of Exhilaration

I suppose all of you are familiar with the name of 'Calcutta Tea Cabin' - Kali Babu's famous tea shop, situated in the gully right behind New Delhi's Gol Market.

It was the evening of Dussera. The time, around seven P.M. The usual crowd consisting of Ram Taran Mukherjee, a retired old gentleman, Kapil Gupta, the school teacher, Bireswar Sinha, the bank clerk, Atul Haldar, the reporter and several others who frequented the tea-shop regularly, were all gathered. The usual Dussera greetings having been exchanged, every one was now busy tucking in. Kali Babu had dreamt up an ultra special menu in honour of the special occasion consisting of fried puffed-rice, pakodas, nimki and gauja, to be washed down with cups of tea.

Atul Haldar remarked that although Kali Babu had provided an extra-special tea he had left out an important item: "If only he had provided a sip of poppy-seed sherbet along with it, things would be just perfect."

"It is quite prepostrous of you to demand poppy-seed sherbet in a tea-shop!" exclaimed Ram Taran, "It wouldn't be the thing at all. All said and done, poppy-seed sherbet which is called 'Bhanga' or 'Vijaya' in Sanskrit - is a sacred drink. Kali Babu's tea-shop is a crowded den, chockful of all kinds of people! How on earth can one possibly taste poppy-seeds here?" 'Vijaya' has to be taken in a pure state of body and mind just when the image of the goddess has been immersed and after one has touched the feet of one's elders as a mark of respect. In fact, I have managed to keep up the old tradition at home. I took a sip just before coming here."

Ram Taran had barely finished talking when a sadhu strode into the tea-shop. He was a six-footer, sturdily-built with a shock of loose hair touching his shoulders. He had a bushy moustache, a rake-like tuft of salt and pepper beard, and a broad forehead liberally smeared with ashes. He wore a chain of rudraksha beads, a saffron-coloured monkey cap, a loose saffron robe and saffron-colour shoes. He carried a huge aluminium urn with a handle. "Good evening, Sirs!" said the sadhu in a booming voice, "I hope you're all doing well?"

"Why, its Mr. Jatadhar Bakshi!" cried Kapil Gupta, "welcome, Sir! Haven't set eyes on you for two whole years! Where had you disappeared all this time? By the way, it looks as though you've gone in for a completely new face-lift! Since when have you turned into a 'sadhu-maharaj' eh? You have got your beard quite beautifully permed! Would you mind telling me how much you had to pay for the job?"

Ram Taran said, "Look here, Jatadhar Bakshi, you've managed to fool us twice in the past. But we're not letting you do it a third time!"

"For goodness sake, let the poor man get back his breath. Listen to what he has to say," cried Kapil Gupta, trying to get a word in edgeways, "you can send for the police later. Kali Babu, please get a plate of snacks and a cup of tea for Mr. Bakshi and charge it to my account."

I wonder if you have seen a famous portrait by Ravi Verma, depicting Menaka with baby Sakuntala in her arms, with Vishwamitra looking the other way, his arm raised in protest. Jatadhar struck a pose almost akin to Vishwamitra's as he said, "Please don't embarrass me any more! You have treated me several times in the past. It is I who owe you a treat this time!" Ram Taran said, "What news of your Achala, eh? That merry widow whom you were supposed to have married the last time you were here?"

Jatadhar heaved a long, long sigh and said, "Please don't mention her name, Mr. Mukherjee! It hurts too much! Achala ditched me in favour of her first husband, Balahari. In fact it was Balahari who dragged her away forcibly from me - her and my fifty-rupees! What's more, he even gobbled up every one of the mutton chops which I had bought for Achala from this very tea-shop!"

Kapil Gupta said, "Oh well, it's no good crying over spilt milk! You'd better tell us how you came to take to the saffron robe instead. No need to feel shy or embarrassed. You can tell us while you eat. We're dying to know what really happened. Kali Babu, please give Mr Bakshi another cup of tea and another plate of snacks. And a couple of Burma cigars as well. Charge it all to me, of course."

Jatadhar took a sip of tea and said, "Oh well, I'll tell you how it happened, since you insist. You see, I was swept by a wave of disenchantment the moment Achala left me and felt quite sick of life! I just threw off everything and joined a band of pilgrims, going right up to Manas Sarovar in Kailash. It is there that I happened to meet Kanhaiya Baba, who, incidentally, used to be Kanai Batabyal before he made up his mind to don the saffron robe. He used to be a brilliant scientist and a leading businessman. But he gave it all up at the dusk of his life and went off to meditate in a Himalayan cave for full five years. I used to know him - though not very intimately - before he turned hermit. What's more, he too recognised me the moment he set his eyes on me! I fell at his feet and told him all that I had suffered and he said, "Don't worry, Jatadhar. Just rid yourself of every worldly desire and become my disciple if you like. I have taken the noble resolution that I shall build a large monastery on the banks of this very Manas Sarovar so that it may provide shelter to pilgrims. I have already got the green signal from the government of Tibet. Dalai Lama, Tasi Lama, Panchen Lama have all sent me their blessings. I shall soon be travelling all over the country to collect funds for my project. You too may accompany me and help my noble cause." I accepted the offer gratefully. In fact I've been travelling with him all over the country ever since - right from the Himalayas to the Kanyakumari. Every one has been contributing for our monastery, the rich and the poor alike. Each according to his ability, of course. So the contributions range from one anna (six paise) to one lakh. We haven't done too badly, either. We've managed to collect around three lakhs and seventy-five thousand rupees so far. We've put it all into the Indo-Tibeten Yaksha Bank. Kanu Maharaj is in Delhi at the moment, putting up with Seth Gajananji at Daryagunj. I took his leave to come and look you up this evening - that's why I'm here."

"But we're, none of us, going to contribute a paisa to your monastery," said Ram Taran, "so you might as well know it from the start! We just don't trust you!"

"Spoken like a true seeker of enlightenment!" said Jatadhar with a beaming smile. "How can I possibly expect you to trust me when you are totally unaware of the great change in me? It was my evil fate which drove me to my destruction, making me a villain in your eyes! Do you think I am not acutely conscious of my past failings? In any case, whenever a person contributes anything to a noble cause, he has to do it respectfully. Specially when it comes to contributing for a monastery. "Shradhyeya deyam," as the saying goes. Why should you contribute to a cause you don't respect? And why should I ask it of you?"

"Thank you, Jatai Maharaj!" said Atul Haldar, "your words are delightfully assuring! I've been feeling pretty apprehensive the moment you mentioned your monastery and was downright scared that you'd demand a contribution on the spot and have us all in jitters with the threat of Kanhaiya Baba's curse, if we refuse! So far as I am concerned, I feel no respect for your project so there can be no question of my contributing to it. Incidentally, what are you carrying in that huge, big urn of yours?"

"Please don't call it an urn," protested Jatadhar. "It is a Rudra Kamandulu. Gajananji had it specially made for Kanu Maharaj at his request. Of course he could do it because be owns an alluminium factory."

"What have you got there?" asked Ram Taran curiously, "seems to be something liquid."

"Well, if you must know, it contains the Elixir of Exhilaration! I've brought it specially for you."

"I've heard of the elixir of life ," said Ram Taran frowning, "what on earth is this elixir of exhilaration?"

"Oh, its a most wonderful drink, Sir! An incredible invention of Kanu Maharaj. Anyone who drinks it feels totally exhilarated and stimulated! Hence the unusual name!"

"You mean it's a liquor of sorts?"

"Heaven forbid!" cried Jatadhar, "Kanu Maharaj never touches intoxicants! Why, he doesn't even take tea! I could tell you what this stimulant contains. In fact I don't really mind your knowing it so long as you keep the formula a dead secret!"

"Don't worry, Mr Bakshi," said Kapil Gupta. "no one except us here shall ever know."

"Well then, listen to me. The drink contains twenty kinds of herbs, twenty different allopathic drugs, twenty varieties of homeopathic globules, twenty types of hakimi and ayurvedic mixtures - such as gold dust and diamond dust - quantities of air particles and atom particles, a whole lot of vitamins and about 250 grams of electricity - all distilled quite specially in a special instrument. According to Kanu Maharaj, it is the original *soma rasa* drunk by the sages in ancient times. He has merely modernized the age-long formula!"

"Well sir, it is exactly what we need this evening!" cried Atul Haldar in an excited voice. "Wasn't I saying just a little while ago that we only needed a sip of poppy-seed sherbet to make our celebrations complete?"

"Look here Atul, you'd better not be in such a mighty hurry," said Ram Taran in a cautious voice. "How can you be sure that Jatadhar's drink is not an intoxicating one?"

Jatadhar bit his long tongue and said, "How could you think such a thing of me, Mr. Mukherjee? Can I possibly bring you an intoxicating drink being a religious man myself! I don't deny that the mixture contains a few poppy seeds but it isn't ordinary opium at all! All its inebrieting properties have been completely neutralised through a highly scientific process.

The ayurvedic science describes the elixir as *"hridya vrishya, balya, medhya."* Which means, drinking it gives an energetic body, sharpened senses, a cheerful state of mind and the total dismissal of all stress and tension. Well, Kapil Babu, why don't you try it a little and see what it's like? But please wash your tea cup first. One has to drink it in a pure form."

Kapil washed his cup as directed and held it before Jatadhar. "Please give me only a wee drop," he said, "and accept this four-anna bit (25 paise) as my share of the contribution for your monastery."

Jatadhar accepted the coin and took off the lid from his 10-kilo-urn. Then he took out a small ladle and ladled out a measureful in Kapil's cup, saying "please drink it respectfully."

Atul said, "Please give me a little too, Jatai Maharaj. Here are two two-anna bits(12 paise)."

Bireswar Sinha followed suit, contributing four annas for a ladleful of the drink. "It tastes quite fantastic!" he said, sipping slowly "somewhat like Coca-cola."

"Don't be a fool!" said Atul. "How can you possibly compare the two? Well, I tasted milk-punch at the Hungarian Embassy the other day and also champagne at the dinner hosted by the French Consul. But I must admit that your elixir of exhilaration beats both hollow! It is a fabulous concoction, Mr. Jatai, being sweet, sour, satly and bitter all at the same time and in just the right proportions. It's pungent too - probably because of the electricity content - sending tiny little shocks at the pit of the stomach! Here, let me have a little more, will you?"

"I'm a patient of arthritis and a little diabetic as well," said Ram Taran in an anxious voice. "I hope this elixir of yours won't aggravate my complaints!"

"Of course not, sir," said Jatadhar in a shocked voice. "How could you think it for a moment? On the contrary, all your illness will disappear if you drink it. Yes, all sickness of the body, depression of the mind, the burning in your heart - everything will vanish just like magic! Come, open your mouth and I shall pour in a ladleful of my elixir. Please drink respectfully, Sir. Drink respectfully and give respectfully!"

"You are a pest, Jatadhar!" said Ram Taran, "An obstinate and infuriating pest, bent on extracting contributions from all! Very well! Here is a whole rupee! Take it as my share of the donation."

Inspired by old Ram Taran's noble example, everyone had a go at the elixir of exhilaration. After gulping down three ladlefuls at one go, Bireswar Sinha burst into tears and said, "I'm terribly unhappy, Jatadharji! My wife insults me day in and day out, calling me a fool, a blockhead and a chump!"

"Never mind, Bireswar Babu," said Jatadhar in a comforting voice, "drink up a little more of the elixir and shed all your misery for good! You are a man, after all, brave and lion-hearted! How dare anybody call you a fool! Come, have another sip, and no one will dare to call you names any more. They'll fear you instead!"

A starry-eyed Ram Taran said, "Your elixir is really wonderful! Here are two rupees. Please give me a generous helping. My wife keeps telling me that I'm a senile old fool! In fact, the wretched female doesn't respect me at all! Too puffed up, because she happens to be a rich man's daughter, though how much of her father's wealth she brought for me is quite another question. I shall deal with her tonight. In fact I already feel quite equal to the task!"

Jatadhar said, "Mr Mukherjee, this elixir of mine contains solar energy, heat energy as well as divine energy! You are a Brahmin after all, pure at heart, belonging to the direct line of sages. All your ancestors performed *soma yajnas!* They must have gulped down buckets of *soma rasa* in the process! You don't need to worry about any kind of energy! Come, let me fill up your cup to the brim. Drink it to the lees! It costs five rupees, by the way. Give respectfully, drink respectfully."

All those who were present in Kali Babu's teashop devoured the Elixir of Exhilaration in varying quantity. But the reaction of the stimulant was quite different on different people! Kapil Gupta suddenly turned grim and muttered lines from 'Macbeth'. Bireswar Sinha and a few others sobbed and whimpered like tiny tots. Some lay flat on the floor and promptly fell asleep. Atul Haldar stood up and waved his arms about, as he dramatically declined lines from 'Shah Jahan.' "Ah Princess! Emperor's daughter! Would you have me fear death?"

Ram Taran squatted on the bench and broke into a lilting 'Ramprasadi' air, beating time with his fingers - "Oh Kali! I shall grab your chopper now. I shall chop off your hanging tongue with devotion and lay it at Lord Siva's feat!"

Kali Babu sat quietly behind his counter, silently observing all that was going on. Now he walked up to Jatadhar and asked, "Well Jatadhar Babu, how much have you managed to grab this evening? A tidy sum, I'll bet!"

"Are you talking about the donation I received for my monastery? Nothing to write home about, I'm afraid! Around rupees fifty or so, at most. None of your clients are exactly people of means! Most of them seem to be living a hand-to-mouth existence!"

"I hope you are aware of the fact that any business done within my shop means paying me a commission?"

"Of course I do! Here is five rupees - a little more than ten percent of my earning."

"Is there any elixir left in that urn of yours?"

"Just a little - about two cups or so. Like to try it?"

"Yes, but I'm not going to pay you anything."

"I wouldn't dream of asking you for payment! Here, drink it all up!"

Kali Babu gulped down two cups of the Elixir of Exhilaration. Almost immediately his eyes grew drowsily dreamy! Jatadhar said, "Come, Kali Babu, lie down on the table and rest for a while. Don't worry! All of you are going to feel thoroughly stimulated before long! Ten minutes flat, in fact! Incidentally, I am slightly short of cash and must borrow some from you. I need it to pay for my journey to the monastery. Rupees twenty-five should be enough, I think. I am taking it from your cashbox, if you don't mind. Do you need a handnote? No? Thank you, Kali Babu! You are a noble man, after all, so why should you mind helping a friend out? Put it down to my account and I shall pay back every paisa - principal as well as the interest - when I come next."

"But when will that be?" asked Kali Babu in a muffled voice, rolling his drowsy eyes.

"That depends entirely on God's will. I shall come whenever Kanhaiya Baba sends for me! So goodbye for now! Better shut the door. You'd be wise to take a little precaution, as there seem to be too many thieves running wild! Good night."

The Creation of Bateswar

Bateswar Sikdar, an ardent devotee of the Goddess of Learning, is a writer by profession. Although most of the writers who take up writing as their sole mode of livelihood, are not too well off, Bateswar happens to be a wealthy man. This exceptional state of affairs is brought about by the fact that he is a first-rate man of letters. And he writes only novels. That too very lengthy ones. Unlike the second and third rate writers, he does not believe in wasting his talents by going in for short stories, articles, poems, skits or travelogues. None of his novels contain less than seven hundred pages. The famished readers of Bengal gobble them up the moment they are out and eagerly await the next one. He has just celebrated his sixty-fifth birthday. Or rather, his readers have done it, with a great deal of fanfare.

One evening, as Bateswar sat writing in his study, sipping tea at intervals from an oversize tea-pot, an unknown young man walked into the room and greeted him. "My name is Priyabrata Ray" said the stranger, "Would you be kind enough to spare me five minutes?"

He was around thirty and had a pleasing appearance. His clothes, though not exactly chic bore no trace of poverty. "Sit down," said Bateswar, pointing to a chair, "I suppose you are bringing out a new magazine and want me to give you a story? Let me tell you right away that I'm no wishing-tree and cannot possibly oblige anyone who happens to ask for articles! I can give you a signed 'Best Wishes', if you like, but mind you, you'll have to shell out ten rupees for it".

"But I haven't come to bother you for contributions", said Priyabrata, "I've merely come to ask you something about that story of yours, 'Who Stays, who Goes,' which is being serialised in *Pragamini* magazine. Could you please tell me for how long it is likely to continue?"

"Another six or seven months at least ," replied Bateswar, "but why do you ask? How do you like the story, eh?"

"It's just wonderful! All the characters seem so real! I feel tremendously curious about the conclusion. That is why I've come to ask you whether the heroine of the story ---that girl named Aloka who is in the sanatorium with tuberculosis -- will eventually get well or not."

Priyabrata's eagerness pleased Bateswar. He smiled and said, "Why should I tell you? A story loses all its charm if the plot is disclosed beforehand."

"Sir, please have mercy on Aloka," pleaded Priyabrata with folded hands. "And please do let her live!"

Your request is downright outlandish, young man," said Bateswar, "why are you so concerned about the heroine of my story, anyway? And there happens to be an equal demand for both tragedy and comedy. The readers want both. Moreover, I can't possibly write my story according to your dictation. If you are so mad about happy endings, go and read my *Tussle* or *Triple pulls* and books like that"

"Have mercy on me, Sir" cried Priyabrata in a pathetic voice.

"You are an absolute nut," said Bateswar looking him up and down. "For goodness' sake, get lost and don't waste my time. Instead of worrying your head over Aloka, go and get yourself properly treated. I'm positive you are a mental case!"

Priyabrata hung down his head and walked out quietly. It was nine-thirty p.m. Bateswar was about to go in for dinner when the telephone rang. He picked up the receiver, saying, "Whom do you want to speak to? Yes, this is Bateswar speaking. Who are you?"

"Good evening," came the answer, " Dr.Sanjeev Chatterjee on the line. I want to see you on an urgent matter. May I come around eight tomorrow morning? Or would I be disturbing you ?"

"Oh no, not at all. You are most welcome," said Bateswar, "but what is the urgent matter all about ?"

"I'll tell you when we meet. Goodnight Sir!"

Bateswar was familiar with Dr.Sanjeev Chatterjee's name. He was young, just returned from the U.K., said to be an excellent surgeon and had already built up a roaring practice.

The doctor turned up punctually. "Good morning, Sir,"he said politely. "I've no intention of wasting your precious time! I'll say all I have to in just ten minutes. Really, Sir, you wield a magic pen ! That story of yours--"Who Stays, who Goes"--which is being serialised in *Pragamini*, is too wonderful for words! You have cast a spell on the entire reading public! And as for folks like Sarat Chandra, Tara Shankar, Banaphool and Prabodh 'Sandal' -- well, you've beaten them all hollow!"

Bateswar smiled. "I hear you have a roaring practice" he said, "How do you find time to read my stories?"

"Well, I just have to make time, Sir", replied the doctor. "I've no choice in the matter! Wherever I go, I hear your story being discussed. Even in our medical club! The other day when I was performing a hernia operation on an old man, he squealed out-- 'Ah, wonderful Aloka! Long live!'-- although he was under anesthesia! Even my relatives are downright crazy about this Aloka of yours. They all say --Bateswar Sikdar is the monarch of fiction. No one else, not even Damodar Laskar, the 'Galpa-Saraswati', can hold a candle to him!"

The doctor paused a second and said --"Let me now speak of my urgent business. I have actually come to ask a favour of you on behalf of all my friends and relatives. Please make your Aloka get well fast, because everyone is getting downright jittery about her condition. Let her return from the sanatorium completely recovered. It should be a thorough cure, mind you! Aloka's husband is a pretty wealthy chap. Let him take her to Simla or Ooty and stay there for three months at least. She can return home once she has put on some weight and looks plump and chubby once again."

Bateswar looked somewhat put out as he replied, "But unfortunately that's not possible Dr. Chatterjee. My story happens to be a tragedy. Aloka is not destined to live!"

"Not destined to live! What on earth do you mean, Sir? Of course she'll live! Nearly 90 percent of T.B. cases get well these days. Just see to it that she is given proper treatment, that's all! Let her take medicines like P.A.S., streptomycin, isonayacide, etc. I could easily fix up an appointment with my friend Dr. Baral if you want further details."

Bateswar was in a real fix. The man who had come

to see him the previous day was mad enough. But today's visitor appeared to be a raving lunatic ! More over, Dr. Sanjeev happened to be a famous man and could not be thrown out rudely. But the doctor's gushing praise as well as uncalled for advice seemed so intolerable to Bateswar that he felt that the best thing for him to do would be to tell him frankly about the intended conclusion of his story.

Bateswar said, "Dr, Chatterjee, you seem to have forgotten one important fact. Aloka is not a real human being. She is merely the heroine of my story. If I allow her to live, my entire novel is going to be ruined! Aloka is slated to die. Two years after her death her husband Hemant is going to marry Sharbari. Sharbari is the other girl in my story -- the one who had been waiting for Hemant for full five years."

Dr. Sanjeev banged the table with his fist, crying, "Absurd! Downright impossible! Aloka's husband belongs to her alone! What right has this other woman to snatch him away?"

"But do try and see Sharbari's role in the story too, Dr. Chatterjee!" said Bateswar, "she is far superior to Aloka in looks, talent, qualifications and of course, health! If she does not get Hemant after waiting for him all these years, well, her heart will break!"

"Break, my foot!" scoffed Dr. Sanjeev, "Hearts don't break that easily, Sir ! It's made up of very strong tissues. And even if her heart happens to be damaged, let her get proper treatment, that's all ! Give her a course of digitalis, aminophylin and similar drugs. Let her apply boric compress on her chest, followed by a mustard plaster and then top it up with an icebag! Why on earth need she get married ? Send her to Raj Kumari Amrit Kaur and she can arrange to get her trained as a nurse instead !"

"Obviously you are so excited about my story that you are taking the imaginary characters to be real ones! I suppose it's a big compliment," said Bateswar tactfully. "But do try and consider the writer's point of view as well ! We have to write stories with happy endings as well as those with tragic ones ! Think of God . He imparts both joy and sorrow, doesn't He ? He protects, as well as destroys. It is He who has made up this life of meetings and partings. We writers merely imitate God in our works. A man might not welcome sorrow in his real life but that does not stop him from relishing a tragedy! That is precisely the reason why all great writers have created characters like Sita, Indumati, Ophelia and Desdemona ! God cannot always he merciful! Neither can we."

"What on earth do you mean, Sir ? And what blasted cheek to imagine that you can possible play God! In any case, God is totally helpless in the matter of showing mercy! Surely you can realise that. He cannot show mercy to all at one and the same time. If He were to be merciful to the mice, the cats would starve. If He were to show mercy to fish, chicken, goats and lambs, you and I would starve. When He is merciful to men, the microbes face destruction. When He chooses to show mercy to the microbes, its the other way round! That is precisely why He has created man --- so that man at least gets the chance to practise non-violence and consider it to be the greatest religion of all. How dare you think that you have the right to go about murdering people just because you happen to be a story-teller?", asked Dr. Sanjeev, fuming. "Forget what Vaimiki, Kalidasa and Shakespeare wrote centuries ago! Remember, this is the age of Gandhiji ! No one has any use for tragedy. In fact, all those who write tragedy and all those who relish them are morbid. And what's more, they have a latent streak of cruelty in them ! We have no dearth of sorrow in real life, so why inflict imaginary ones as well ? Give joy and happiness and not a load of tear-jerkers ! Make your readers laugh. And why need you worry? You can create, keep or destroy with a mere stroke of your pen, can't you? Well, to cut it short, you simply must make Aloka live --do you understand ? Sir Conan Doyle had also killed off his Sherlock Holmes. But the storm of protests from his readers made him resurrect the chap once again ! Why on earth can't you do the same ?"

Annoyed and exasperated at this uncalled for lecture, Bateswar said, "Excuse me, Dr. Chatterjee, but I don't agree with you. We, laymen, don't go about telling you how you should treat your patients, do we? So I fail to see why you should bother us with your opinions. And that too uncalled for ones ! Minding other people's business isn't good for either of us !"

Dr. Sanjeev stood up and said, "It is my business! It is a doctor's duty to save lives. You are about to commit murder, so I thought that it is my duty to protest. But have it your own way. But your six lakh readers - four lakh female ones amongst them - are not going to forgive you in a hurry. You may even have to pay for this folly in your next life ! And I warn you, Sir, you'd better be a little careful in your movements. The youngsters of today are not given to taking things lying down ! And do send for me in case of broken bones. Goodbye."

Dr. Sanjeev quite spoilt Bateswar's mood. He seemed to be a giddy-headed drunken boor. Bateswar wondered how such a weird character had managed to become such a successful surgeon. In any case, he was not given to being affected by the rantings of a madman. He was not going to change the plot of his story - and that was that ! But he decided to be a little careful in his movements in view of Dr. Sanjeev's warnings.

The Creation of Bateswar   41

Three days later Bateswar sat smoking his cigar in his balcony. His rheumatic pain was worse and it was rather difficult for him to keep climbing stairs. His wife was away at Benares, visiting her sister and had taken the children with her. There was not a soul to speak to. Bateswar was bored and longed for a visit from one of his friends or admirers. Just then a servant came up and informed him that there was a lady to see him downstairs. "Bring her up here" said Bateswar at once. A young woman of about twenty-four stepped daintily into the balcony. She was undoubtedly pretty though rather on the heavy side. She bent down and touched his feet respectfully. "That will do" said Bateswar hastily, "Who are you ?"

"Can't you really recognise me ?" said the lady in an astonished voice, "why, I am Kadambanila ! Surely you must have seen me on the silver screen ? I may not be a superstar as yet but I am very much in demand, I assure you. I am regarded as the most promising amongst the rising stars."

"I am very glad to know it", said Bateswar hastily, "but you see, I hardly ever see films, so I know very little about stars and that sort of thing. But don't keep standing. Take that chair over there."

"Oh you don't need to be so formal with me, Sir," said Kadambanila chewing a betel leaf - a fact which rather annoyed Bateswar at first. What audacity ! But he was somewhat soothed by her polite tone. well, at least she isn't smoking in my presence, he told himself thankfully. Then he looked at her and said, "Kadambanila must be your screen name. Please tell me what your real name is."

"I can't, Sir" said Kadambanila, "You see, filmstars and hermits are not supposed to disclose their true identity. Their gurus forbid them to utter it again. But

I suppose you find it somewhat difficult to pronounce my name. You may call me 'Kadu' if you like."

"Of course not !" said Bateswar annoyed. "I can't possibly call you Kadu ! I'd much rather address you by your full name. Now, tell me. why have you come to see me ?"

Kadambanila leaned back against the chair, closed her eyes and said in a melting voice, "Ah Grandpa, what a magnificent story you have written ! I'm talking of the one which is being serialised in *Pragamini* - "Who Stays, who Goes". Everyone I know is simply raving about it ! All of us feel that such a masterpiece has never appeared in Bengali literature before ! Now, I have come to you with a business proposal. This story is sure to be a blockbuster if filmed. Lala Nebuchand is willing to spend upto ten lakhs to get it done. He has naturally asked me to be the heroine of the film. We intend to ask Debaki Bose - or some other equally competent director - to direct our film. Lalaji will pay you ten thousand or more for the story. He is going to pay me quite well too. Now, I only hope you will agree to the proposal ."

Bateswar was outright delighted. "Why shouldn't I agree ?" he said with a smile, "you will look quite beautiful as the heroine, I'm sure. But the story will take another seven months to complete, you know."

"Never mind, Grandpa. I too have several engagements at the moment. I shall remain extremely busy in Bombay for the next seven months. So will Nebuchandji, for that matter. He merely wants your consent at the moment. He is going to finalise the deal and draw up the agreements after your story is complete. In the mean time, don't you promise to give the story to any other party." "Of course not!" said Bateswar.

"You will see how wonderfully I play Aloka's role.

I just love the character. When she appears in the last scene, plump and bonny, holding her three-month old baby in her arms, the theatre will simply ring with applause ! And if you happen to be present at the premere show, the audience will lift you up on their shoulders and dance for joy !"

Bateswar groaned in exasperation . "Oh no !" he said in an impatient voice, "not you too ! You will turn me crazy, between the lot of you ! Look here, Kadambanila, this story of mine happens to be a tragedy, see? Aloka is destined to die. Two years later her husband Hemant is going to marry Sharbari."

Kadambanila's eyebrows shot up in horror. "What!" she cried in a shocked voice, "so you intend to kill off Aloka, do you ? In that case I wash my hands off the whole affair !"

"Don't be absurd !" said Bateswar, "one can act equally well as the heroine of a tragedy ."

"No way !" said Kadambánila in an obstinate voice, "I absolutely refuse to die ! Even as Aloka ! Really Grandpa, It's too bad of you to dash all my hopes like this ! I see that mine has been a fool's errand and that I've wasted your time for nothing. I'd better go and see Damodar Galpa Saraswati instead. Perhaps I can get him to agree to our proposal. I think his novel 'The Mental Serpent' is quite fascinating and I also like the character of Manjula who is the heroine of the story. It is a very good role."

Bateswar grew visibly restless at her words. Only a few days ago the callow critic of the popular magazine Dundubhi had written, "Damodar Naskar's stories are full of present day awareness - both social and political and sex appeal, whereas Bateswar Sikdar's stories are totally non-significant, pointless, boring and repetitive." As a result , Bateswar felt mad at the very mention of Damodar's name. He waved his hands excitedly and cried, "Don't you dare go to that oaf ! What's the tearing hurry ? Give me a couple of days to consider whether I can make Aloka live after all."

"But there is no time for consideration, Grandpa" said Kadambanila shaking her head. "I have to dash off to Bombay first thing tomorrow morning. I have to take a final decision today and tell Nebuchandji about it."

Bateswar paused thoughtfully, his hand on his cheek. Finally he said, "Oh very well. Have it your way. I shall have to let Aloka live and make Sharbari die instead ! You need not approach anyone else for a story. Let me tell you one thing, Kadambanila. We writers are omnipotent ! We can make or unmake characters with a stroke of our pen !"

In a moment Kadambanila was all smiles. "Thank you, Grandpa," she said in a jovial voice. "That's like a good boy ! Let me touch your feet. But you must make the conclusion a really happy one. Please ensure that Aloka appears in the last scene with her baby son in her arms. In the mean time, I shall go to Nebuchandji and tell him the good news."

Bateswar Sikdar did keep his promise. His novel 'Who Stays, who Goes' ended on a happy note. But there was no trace of Kadambanila after her initial visit more than eight months ago. Bateswar did not know her address so he could not even contact her.

A few days later, as Bateswar sat writing a brand new story - 'The Tug - of -War of Hearts'- he heard a familiar voice ask -"May we come in, Mr. Sikdar ?"Almost immediately Dr. Sanjeev Chatterjee walked into the room, followed by Priyabrata and an unknown girl. "Good morning, Sir" said Dr. Sanjeev, "oh that story of yours is a truly wonderful creation, I must say. By the way, I hope you recognise this gentleman, Priyabrata Ray, whom you had dismissed as a looney ! And this is Aloka, whose life you have actually saved."

Aloka bent down and touched Bateswar's feet. Then she laid a large container wrapped in tissue paper on the table. "Aloka has made these delectable curd sweets specially for you," said Dr. Sanjeev, "please taste them, Sir"

Bateswar looked totally bewildered as he said, "But what's all this ? I don't understand what you're trying to say. "I'll tell you, Sir" said Dr. Sanjeev with a broad smile, "this is the real and true conclusion of your story. I'll explain how it all happened. Aloka here, who is Priyabrata's wife, also happens to be my wife's sister. Now, Aloka was in the sanatorium for a year or so, responding wonderfully to the treatment there. In fact, she was very nearly recovered when, as ill luck would have it, a copy of *Pragamini* fell into her hands. As she read your story she developed a queer complex and started saying that if the Aloka in your story lives, she would live too. But if Aloka died, so would she. She was in dead earnest, mind you ! We tried our utmost to convince her that it was sheer madness on her part and that she should not allow a trashy story to upset her like this ! Specially since she was nearly well again. But Aloka's queer notion persisted and turned into a regular obsession. So her husband - Priyabrata here - tried to reason with you. But you simply called him a nut and threw him out. Then I came along and gave you a regular lecture. But I merely succeeded in putting your back up ! Then my wife said, 'You fellows are absolute good-for-nothings ! Unsuited for the simplest of jobs ! I'd better go and tackle the old man myself.' So she came along and got you to change your plot in just five minutes ! Your changed story enabled Aloka to recover double quick. Just see how plump she has now grown !"

"But the lady who came to see me was the film star Kadambanila," protested Bateswar.

"No one in her family has ever acted in films," said Dr. Sanjeev laughing, "not in the last seven generations! That was my wife Anila who bluffed you by pretending to be Kadambanila. A real sly creature, Sir! Anyway, please bless the real Aloka now."

"Yes, of course," said Bateswar, "Aloka dear, may you have a long and happy life. May God bless you with good and worthy children and may the Goddess Lakshmi be ever present in your home !" He paused for a moment and said, "Well, Doctor, I see it all now. But why didn't your wife - Anila or Kadambanila, whatever her name might be - come along too ?"

"How can she, Sir ?" said Dr. Sanjeev with twinkling eyes, "she is in the nursing home at the moment with a baby son who weighs full ten pounds ! Let her come home first. I'm sure she will come over to beg your pardon for having bluffed you the other day !"

The Celestial Strip-tease

"What on earth are you playing at, Urvashi?" said Indra, the King of Heaven. "You are literally rolling in happiness in this Paradise of ours! You have a lovely villa, an exquisite garden, expensive clothes, jewellery, to speak nothing of a whacking fat salary! You've been enjoying all this to the brim. So, why on earth do you want to throw it all up and go down to the earth instead? King Pururava is no longer alive, as you know very well. Which means, there is no one down there who is likely to wait on you, hand and foot. Besides, you may enjoy eternal youth here in Paradise and flaunt your unblemished looks holding all the angels and also their King captive but please remember that once you go down on earth, you're going to be an old hag in no time! Once that happens, no one is likely to give you a second glance - no matter how many layers of cosmetics you slap on!"

Urvashi bowed her head low and said, "Oh Heavenly Sovereign, I am totally fed up of Paradise! I have already conquered every single male in this establishment so their boring sychophancy does not turn me on any more. If I go down to the earth, I am sure to get a number of fresh admirers and any amount of money. In case I happen to find myself aging - well, I can always come back, can't I?"

"You've become exceedingly conceited, thats what!" said Indra, "you can't really have any dearth of admirers here!"

"Perhaps not. But I shall get many more on earth! Human beings are far more interesting. Just listen to what a human poet has written about me-

'Sages, waking up from their meditation
Offer the fruits of their prayers at thy feet!
Urvashi, a mere glance from thine eyes
Turns the three worlds restless!'

Is there a single poet in Paradise who can write lines like these?"

"All poets write nothing but lies!" grunted Indra. "In any case, I shall agree to let you go if you can actually prove to me that you have conquered each and every man here. What about the great sages and the ascetics? Can you win them over too?"

"Pooh!" said Urvashi. "Every one of them fell a victim to my charms, ages ago!"

"Very well. I shall put it to test. Have you heard of the divine men who are able to roam freely in both heaven and earth? I mean, people like Sanat Kumar, Sanatan, Sanak and Sadananda? They are the soul-creations of Lord Brahma himself. But I'd rather not involve them in this matter. All of them have vile tempers! But three other sages have recently come here on a visit - Kutuk, Parvat and Kardam. They seem to be fairly mild and totally indifferent to all earthly things. Do you think you could conquer them?"

"Why not? That is, if they are men!"

"Not just men - they're all super men!"

"Then I shall acheive a super-victory over them!" said Urvashi in an arch voice.

"Very well. We shall see. They are friends of sage Narada. I shall invite them to my court to witness your dance."

The three sages were delighted to learn about the invitation. They told Narada, "You know, we have seen peacocks dancing and butterflies dancing. We have also seen the dance of monkeys and bears. It will be a completely new experience to see a woman dance! But they say this Urvashi is a nymph. We hope she is a woman as well?"

"Of course she is a woman," said Narada, "a woman, at the sight of whom the heart of man grows restless and the blood turns aflame! You'll be charmed by her performance, I'm sure! Now, get ready to visit Indra's court."

Parbat's beard reached up to his neck, Kardam's up to his chest and Kutuk's beard reached right down to his knees. Each got-dressed according to his own requirement of decency. Parbat wore a bark. Kardam could not find one so he just wore a loin-cloth. Kutuk had no inhibitions at all. Besides, he possessed neither bark nor loin-cloth. So he calmly chose to wear nothing. "Look here, Kutuk," said Narad eying him, "You'd better wear a grass- skirt at least!"

"What for?" said Kutuk, "can't you see my knee-length beard? I don't need clothes to cover myself!" Indra greeted the sages respectfully, offering them the usual tokens of respect. Then he found seats for them and said, "Oh you all-powerful sages, who have achieved total fulfilment in your meditation and attained complete control over your senses, Urvashi, the chief amongst my nymphs, will perform an unique dance for your entertainment. It is called the 'Nirmoke

Nritya.' People on earth - particularly those in western countries - call it the 'strip-tease'. Our guests today are all famous personalities. We have with us here, all the important gods - such as, the fire-god and the rain-god - important sages, such as Narada and hermits like Agastya. Menaka and other well known nymphs are also here. We are all highly honoured by your presence. Now, with your kind permission, I would like to call upon Urvashi to begin her dance."

Kutuk, the mouthpiece of the three guests, said, "Yes, please do. No point in unnecessary delay when we've all been specifically invited to see the dance."

Urvashi, donning a loose robe over her tantalisingly provocative dance costume, entered the court of Indra and bowed low to convey her respects to all. Then she folded her hands and said, "Respectful devas and supremely powerful sages, the dance which I am going to perform will involve the gradual revelation of my body. I hope you won't consider it objectionable?" "Of course not," said Kutuk shaking his head and huge beard at one and the same time, "what is there to object to?" Your body too is composed of the five elements, just like the body of any other living creature! What we want to see is the essence of womanhood concealed deep within."

Urvashi bowed. "In case you find anything ugly or obscene in my dance, please tell me and I shall modify my steps immediately." She then threw off her loose robe and revealed the flashy costume underneath on which gold, pearls and precious gems glimmered and glittered, dazzling the eyes of the beholders. After dancing for a while Urvashi also throw off the veil which covered the upper part of her torso. Sage Parbat raised his hand in protest. "Stop Urvashi," he cried "your dance is extremely immodest! We've no wish to see these indecent and soul-harrassing gyrations of yours!"

"Who cares about your soul-harrassment?" said sage Kutuk annoyed. "If you can't stand the dance, then for goodness' sake, close your own eyes! The rest of us want to see it."

Urvasi glided up to Indra and whispered, "I've conquered Parbat, Sire!"

The dance continued. Sage Parbat covered his eyes with both his hands but curiosity got the better of him and he watched her through the gaps in his fingers.

Urvashi soon uncovered the entire upper half of her body. "Stop!" cried sage Kardam, covering his eyes. "The fruits of all our years of meditation shall be utterly undone if we continue to watch this lustful dance of yours! Stop, for heaven's sake!"

Kutuk scolded him soundly! "Why on earth should she stop? If you can't stand it, get lost yourself!" Urvashi smiled and winked at Indra to tell him that Kardam was under her spell too.

Eventually Urvasi threw off every garment and jewellery which adorned her body and stood all bare like a beautiful statue made of alabaster. All the devas and sages present in the court cried, "Bravo Urvashi! Well done!"

But Kutuk still looked puzzled and said, "Why have you stopped, Urvashi? Come on, shed more clothes!"

"But she has nothing more to shed," said Narada,

"She has already shed all that she wore."

"What about that lotus-like garb all over her body?" asked Kutuk.

"Good God! That's her skin!"

"Well, ask her to shed it!"

"Are you mad, Kutuk?" said Narada. "The skin is a part of her body. It is not an external garment!"

"It may not be a garment but it is a covering, all the same. Why can't she take it off? I want to see what lies beneath," said Kutuk.

"Well, I can tell you what lies beneath," said Narada. "There are layers of fat just under the skin, then the muscles and finally the skeleton."

"What lies beneath the skeleton?"

"Nothing at all," said Narada.

"Nothing?" cried Kutuk. "Then where is that essential womanhood which turns a man's heart restless and sets his heart ablaze?"

"The womanhood lies in her clothes, her jewellery, her body, her gestures and finally in the eyes and the heart of her lover! You've no feeling at all, Kutuk, and you've turned your heart to ashes! That is why you can't see it!" said Indra.

Kutuk, enraged by his words, cried, "Why did you call me then, if you just meant to bluff me like this? This Urvashi is just like any other soul-less animal! What is the difference between her body and that of a she-goat? Come along, Parbat and Kardam, let's get going. There is nothing to discover here!"

Menaka, Ghritachi, Misrakeshi and the other nymphs, who were all fierce rivals of Urvashi, were delighted at her humiliation and clapped their hands the moment the three sages left the court.

"Don't cry, Urvasi," said Indra "No one can conquer everybody! Remember, I was also defeated by Vritrasura."

"Do you call this defeat, my Lord?" cried Urvasi.

"This Kutuk of yours is no man! He is a useless, senseless lunatic! How could you allow a creature like him to insult me like this in the open court? I shall neither live in your Paradise nor will I go down to the earth. I'll take to the saffron robe instead!"

Urvashi, did eventually cut off her tresses. She also donned a necklace of tulasi seeds, smeared snadalwood paste on her forhead and sought refuge at the feet of Lord Vishnu.

Scholar Dambaru

Sage Rohit sent for his disciple. "Dambaru, my child," he said, "you have already mastered every wisdom on earth. What's more, in spite of having graduated, you have put in ten full years of post graduate research. Your youth is very nearly spent! So, why waste your time with me any more? Better say goodbye to your life of asceticism and take up the life of a householder, as befits your age!"

Dambaru touched his teacher's feet respectfully and laid a tiny piece of gold upon them. "I am a very poor man, my Lord" he said humbly, "but please oblige me by accepting this meagre token of my respect." Rohit laid his hand affectionately on Dambaru's head and said, "Well my boy, the very fact that you have served me faithfully for the last twenty - five years is more than adequate payment. I need no tokens. I know that your means are meagre, so please keep the piece of gold for your own use. I am sure it will come handy during your return journey."

"Respected Sir, you have been kinder than kind to me" said Dambaru, "but could I beg for just a little more knowledge before I depart ?"

Rohit burst out laughing at his words. "My dear

boy, you are already brimful of knowledge - like an overful pitcher! I assure you, your mind is quite incapable of holding even a drop more. What you should do now is to go and find a talented king, impress him with your knowledge and then become either his court scholar or court poet. But steer clear of pompous, self-conceited fools. Don't accept anything from them even if they offer it."

Dambaru nodded and folded his hands respectfully. "Do please give me a title at least," he implored.

"What title would you like to have?" asked the sage curiously.

"If you think me worthy, please give me the title of *Vidyamahodadhi*."

"So be it" said Rohit with a smile." My dear scholar Dambaru, *Vidyamahodadhi*, may you meet with success wherever you go. May the Goddess Saraswati save you and may Brihaspati, the teacher of the devas, bless you with sound knowledge."

Dambaru started on his homeward journey, composing a regal 'Address' all his way. He soon came to know that Vitardana, the king of Kashi, was a highly esteemed king. Dambaru made up his mind to seek refuge at his court. On landing up there Dambaru read out his freshly composed 'Address' to the king:

"*Your glory makes the sun and moon seem dim*
Defeated foes just flee when you're around
The Devas are depressed and lose their vim
and Indra is far too dazed to make a sound!
The nymphs walk out of parasdise so fair
And now they dance around you all day long
Goddess Lakshmi has you in her care
So Vishnu weeps in heaven all alone!
Thus, in praise, I sing this song to ye
Tell me, king, what your command may be?"

Vitardana, highly gratified at his words, said, "It is a marvellous address! Cashier, please give a hundred gold coins to this remarkable Brahmin scholar."

"Sorry, Your Highness" said Dambaru shaking his head, "but I can't accept a gift from a smug and conceited fool!"

"Indeed !" said the astonished king. "And who are you calling a smug, conceited fool, eh ?"

"Yourself, of course !"said Dambaru. "My address is chockful of exaggeration of the grossest kind and yet you've glibly accepted it as your due. And that too with a perfectly straight face! Who else but a fool would do such a thing ?"

Vitardana, seething with rage, cried, "You are a smug old fool yourself! If only you hadn't been a Brahmin I'd have had you impaled for impertinence! Cashier, give this blockhead a piece of silver and throw him out."

Dambaru left without accepting the silver coin and resumed his journey. After travelling a long, long way he reached the city of Kaushambi, the capital of the Vatsas. He walked up to the court of King Puranjay and recited the very same address to him. "What an exquisite piece of composition !" said Puranjay, impressed. "Cashier, give this learned scholar a hundred gold coins."

Dambaru shook his head as he had done on the previous occasion and said, "Sorry, Sire, but my revered teacher has specifically asked me not to accept gifts from smug, conceited fools. So I cannot accept your generous offer. My address is nothing but outlandish sychophancy from beginning to end. And yet you've been foolish enough to accept it as your due !" Puranjay, hopping mad at his words, cried, "You foolish ass of a Brahmin, didn't you know that all addresses meant for God, kings and sweethearts are bound to be exaggerated ? That is what's known as poetic license. I had merely judged your address from the artistic point of view and was least bothered about its contents. Cashier, hand out a silver coin to this unmitigated dunce and throw him out of my court !" Dambaru walked out without accepting the coin. He continued his journey, reaching Dasharna after a long trudge. He went to see Udayudha, the king of the land, and recited the same address.

But strangely enough, Udayudha was raging mad on hearing it. "You liar ! You sychophant ! How dare you insult my credibility by uttering all these gross exaggerations ! Clear out of my kingdom this instant. " "Bravo ! Bravo !" cried Dambaru, beside himself with joy, "May Your Highness be ever victorious! You have passed my test with flying colours. You did not accept my gross exaggerations as truth. Which proves that you are neither conceited nor a fool. But I must say that you are rather aggressive. But never mind that. I have quite made up my mind to grace your kingdom for good. So please make all the necessary arrangements for my setting up a household here. Sanction me a fitting salary so that I may be able to live comfortably and also find a suitable bride for me. I have made up my mind to get married and live the life of a house-holder."

Udayudha burst into a peal of loud guffaws and said, "I like your cheek, you foolish oaf ! How dare you try to test me ! I have no intention of offering refuge to an impertinent old liar like yourself ! Treasurer, hand ten silver coins to this raving lunatic and get rid of him."

So Dambaru was pushed off once again. He had already exhausted all his money acquired by the selling of his gold piece. He possessed nothing else. He reached the kingdom of Malwa at dusk, famished and nearly dead with fatigue. He stood on the bank of the Shipra river, muttering aloud "How unfortunate I am!" he said aloud "My method of testing the kings proved totally useless. Besides, two of the kings were indeed fools! The only one that wasn't, threw me out without any rhyme or reason. What on earth am I to do now ? Oh Goddess of Knowledge. I beseech you, have mercy on me."

Dambaru sat on the river bank and prayed to Goddess Saraswati with all his heart. All of a sudden a sweet voice called out to him, saying, "Are you in danger, Sir?" Dambaru started and opened his eyes to find a bathing beauty in dripping clothes standing right before him. Dambaru sat up and immediately fell at her feet crying, "I bow to thee, Goddess. Oh please save me from my plight."

The maid, however, broke into peals of silvery laughter and said, "Dear me ! I'm not a Goddess at all! I am just Shilindhri, the flower-girl. I make flower ornaments and sell them to the ladies in the palace. I was just getting out of the water after my dip when I saw you looking so dismal and unhappy. Please tell me what the matter is" Dambaru told her his story. "I am Dambaru, the great scholar. I am a dear disciple of Acharya Rohit and hold the title of *"Vidyamahodadhi"*. Sage Rohit is as great as the sage Brihaspati himself. I left his shelter recently because he told me that I was fully qualified and was literally brimming over with knowledge. He also asked me to impress a great king and become his court scholar. But he also told me that I should neither associate with egoistic fools nor accept any gift from them. I took his advise and went to visit the kings of Kashi, Vatsya and Dasharna, one after the other. I tried to test them and soon discovered that the first two were conceited fools and the third, in spite of being a wise man, is exceedingly impertinent and hot tempered. He turned down my offer of residing with him. I am famished, exhausted and haven't a coin to bless myself with. So I cannot decide what I should do."

"Never mind" said Shilindhri in a soothing voice, "please come with me to my cottage. You can have a proper meal and then take rest. You need not hesitate to come with me because my aged mother is there too. You can meet the king of Avanti tomorrow. He is a very wise king. I am sure he will be pleased to look after you."

"Fair Maid," said Dambaru, quite overcome by her words, "that's very kind of you, but I'd rather meet the king today itself. I have to see what he is like. I shall accept your kind hospitality only if I succeed in my mission. If I dont, I shall fast unto death, worshipping Goddess Saraswati."

"Very well, Sir" said Shilindhri, "but would you mind telling me how exactly you tested all these kings?" Dambaru told her the whole story in vivid details. Shilindhri burst out laughing. "You know, Sir, you didn't succeed because you told them sweet falsehoods. Now, the king of Avanti is extremely sharp and a real connoisseur of talent. Go and tell him the truth - his virtues as well as his faults. That should do the trick."

"Your advice seems quite valid, Fair One," said Dambaru thoughtfully. "I tried false praise three times and failed to gain my object. It is worth while seeing what telling the truth might do. But unfortunately I know nothing about the king. And I don't have the least idea about either his faults or his virtues. So, how, I ask you, am I to tell him the truth ?"

"Oh don't you worry about that," said Shilindhri at

once.. "I shall tell you all that you need to know about him. He will come for the evening session of his court at dusk. I shall take you there myself."

Shilindhri briefed Dambaru all the way. Finally she pointed to a cottage amidst a cluster of trees and said -"That's my house - the tiny little one at the left. This road leads straight to the palace gate. Just follow it and you will be there." Shilindhri bade him adieu and left for her house.

King Vikramaditya sat in his royal court in the city of Avanti (now known as Ujjain). Having finished all important work at the morning session, he had just walked into the evening court-session for a brief spell of relaxation and entertainment. Just then Dambaru entered the court with his dishevelled hair, dirty clothes and dirty body. Since he had the obvious looks of a Brahmin scholar no one tried to stop him. He stood before the king and lifted his hand to bless him but no words came to his lips.

The king took a careful look at him and said,-"Dear scholar, you appear to be greatly exhausted. Please go and have a bath and a drink of milk. You can rest awhile after that and when you really feel better come and tell me all you want to say. Treasurer, please take him to our rest house and attend to his needs."

But Dambaru shook his head. "Your majesty" he said to the king, "I have made a solemn vow that I shall not break my fast unless I am able to please you with the address I have just composed for you. So kindly listen to what I have to say:

"Oh brave and mighty king, God-sent
Your subjects live in great content
The good ones thrive on tasty food
The bad ones are impaled for good.
Wise men, scholars, all serve you

And with them, you have yes-men too.
The nine gems, all with world wide fame
Though some are glass-bits, false their fame !
You have three queens, well-loved, astute
And ten fab dancer-paramours cute.
And yet, old king, you're no clean sage !
Why lust for Shilindhri at your age ?
Dambaru, scholar, I speak the truth
Be it pleasant or uncouth.
I speak what folks confide in me-
Now tell me what your wish might be ?"

King Vikramaditys's face turned a deep crimson when he heard Dambaru's address. He turned to his Nine Gems and asked them what they thought about it. Vetala was the first to speak. "Your Majesty, this blockhead deserves to have his head shaved and curd smeared on his cleaned pate. Then he should be placed on a donkey and thrown out of the kingdom."

"What do you suggest, Kalidasa ?"asked the king.

"Please permit me to take Dambaru indoors for awhile, Your Majesty"said Kalidasa, "I shall bring him back after I have spoken to him."

King Vikramaditya gave his consent. Kalidasa took Dambaru's hand and said, "Come with me, scholar."But Dambaru shook his head obstinately and said, "I am not going to budge an inch from here unless I know what the king's intentions are."

"Of course he is pleased with you"whispered Kalidasa, "but I have to explain it all to you properly." Dambaru left the place with him.

Kalidasa returned after a couple of hours. Two of the royal attendants dragged Dambaru between them and placed him before the king in a half-lying posture. Dambaru's body was scrubbed clean of dust. His hair glistened with oil. His tummy was well-bloated and his eyes half-shut. The king looked at him anxiously and asked - "What on earth is wrong with the fellow ?"

"Nothing to be worried about, Your Majesty" said Kalidasa with a smile, "our scholar was over - exhausted with his long journey and total starvation during the period. That is why he had lost his head. He has just had a bath and put on a fresh set of clothes. He has also made a hearty meal at my request. But as a result of having eaten too much after too long he seems to have lost his ability for walking. At the same time, he is very keen that you should hear his final words - right now."

"Very well. Let him say it."

"But he has a problem, Your Majesty. He has eaten such a lot of curd, puffed rice, bananas and laddoos that he seems to have lost his speech temporarily. If you permit me, I shall be his spokesman and tell you what he wants to say."

King Vikramaditya granted him permission. Kalidasa told him all about Dambaru's past history, adding, "This man might be a great scholar, but he also happens to be extremely simple and gullible. What's more, he seems totally ignorant about human nature. Before he turned up at the court he was unfortunate enough to come across Shilindhri, the flower-girl. Now, that mischievous, impertinent, scattered -brained, loose-tongued female stuffed him up with all kinds of stories which Dambaru gulped wholesale and repeated them like a parrot at the court."

"Has Dambaru realised his mistake now ?" asked the king.

"Of course, Your Majesty," said Kalidasa. "He also asked me to tell you that it is because he did not have any first hand knowledge about you that he took Shilindhri's words to be absolute truth. Now, after eating his fill, he has come to the conclusion that it is indeed foolish to be guided by somebody else's opinion. He is very keen to stay on here and get to know you as you really are. He then intends to compose a proper address for you, speaking the actual truth this time. Please grant him his wish and allow him to stay on."

"But what can he possibly do in my court?" asked the king amazed.

"We do not have a court-jester. Please let Dambaru have the post."

"Good heavens, are you crazy, Kalidasa? This man is as dry as timber! I am sure he does not even know the meaning of jest!"

"But he has the innate ability to create humour without even being aware of it - as he did this morning. I am sure he will continue to entertain everyone at the court."

The king burst out laughing. "That seems a good idea!" he said. "Well, scholar Dambaru, I am making you our court jester. Poet Kalidasa will speak to the ministers and arrange for a suitable house and salary for you." Dambaru was already beginning to feel better. He opened his eyes, staggered and finally stood up and said, "Victory to the mighty Vikramaditya! Your Majesty, I have yet another request. Before I left my teacher's hermitage he had asked me to marry and settle down. Please be kind enough to find a bride for me. She should be a well-bred, good-natured, humble-minded and polite girl - that's all I ask for."

Vikramaditya sent for his chief minister. "Beerbhadra, please find a suitable bride for our jester and see to it that the wretched flower-girl who sells her flower-ornaments to my queens is properly punished. Shave off her head, pour curd all over it, shove her atop a donkey and throw her out of my kingdom."

"Oh do please forgive the poor, innocent, helpless and foolish girl, Your Majesty," cried Dambaru, greatly upset.

"I might. But on one condition. I shall forgive her only if Dambaru agrees to marry the impertinent creature !"said the king.

Needless to say, Dambaru agreed at once.

The Two Lions

Becharam Sarkar happens to be a very rich man. He had managed to earn millions during the war by working as a contractor. Not much of his business is in existence at the moment. But Becharam is not worried about that. His greed for money is not umlimited and he knows when to draw the line. He is quite content with what he has managed to save. In fact, he feels greatly relieved to be rid of all his business worries for good.

Becharam is not highly educated. His wife Subala is also an old fashioned, rustic-minded dame. She reads a few novels at times but most of the time cannot make out what they're all about. Their two children, Sumanta and Sumitra, are college-goers. Both of them have modern tastes and are rather ashamed of their parents and their old-fashioned ways. In fact, they rebuke their parents quite openly, saying "Father has merely been concerned with earning money all his life. The only people he knows belong to the business class - Punjabis, Gujaratis, Marwaris and the various officers dealing in trade. He knows nothing whatsoever about culture or heritage. And mother is merely occupied with goldmiths and getting loads of jewellery made. And of course her sheafs of paan and tobacco!"

They often tell their parents, " Father, do get rid of your archaic drooping mustaches and learn to back-brush your hair. You're not really old. Do try to be a little smart, for goodness' sake! And mother, your teeth are a real sight! Excessive betel leaves and nuts have made them as black as the seeds of a custard-apple! You'd better have them all extracted and get new ones. Father has retired from work, so you both have ample time to change your ways. Do try to make yourselves fit for the modern civilized society!"

Becharam and Subala were most obedient parents. They laughed outright at the accusing words of their children and said, "Oh very well! We've brought you up all these years, educated you, and so on. Now you both can bring us up and teach us how to be modern!"

Probably you are familiar with the name of the famous club 'Sajjan Sangati.' Kapot Guha, Bar-at-Law, the secratary of the said club and his wife, Shinjini Guha, were known to Sumanta and Sumitra. They begged the couple to take charge of their parents and polish them up to suit the modern times. Kapot agreed to take on the modernisation of Becharam and Shinjini agreed to polish up Subala. Becharam was no miser. He proposed a handsome salary for both their teachers which Kapot accepted after the usual show of reluctance demanded by courtesy. The Guhas tried to reform everything about the place - interior decorations, meal patterns, clothes, jewellery and etiquette. Becharam got rid of his moustache and brushed back his hair. He even took to wearing pyjamas inside the house instead of the usual dhoti. But Subala refused to give up her betel-and-tobacco chewing. Nor would she agree to having her teeth extracted. Moreover, her rustic accents remained in spite of all Shinjini's efforts.

Becharam had built a grand new house on the Bimbisara Road recently. The plan of the house was suggested by Kapot Guha. A few days after the housewarming party Sumanta told his father, "Let's have a party! All your relatives, business cronies and contractors have already had a grand feed the other day, so there's absolutely no need to call them again. Let's only invite a few select people."

Becharam said, "Well son, I don't know any aristocrats or social elites so I can't possibly shove myself on to them and ask them to my party. Of course I do know a few ministers and deputy-ministers. I could invite them if you want me to. What does Mr. Guha say?"

Kapot Guha said, "Oh well, you needn't worry about the aristocrats right now. In a few days' time they themselves will be eager to make your acquaintance. What I suggest is, have a party for the famous literary stalwarts and make it a real classy affair. If you can arrange for a couple of lions, the rest will eagerly follow suit."

"Good heavens, Mr Guha! How on earth am I to get hold of lions? Talk sense!"

"You have misunderstood me, sir. By 'lion' I meant a famous personality, one whom every one is eager to meet."

Sumanta said, " A lioness would be even better. If, only, you could get hold of a couple of first class film stars, such as Hladini Mandal or Morali Banerjee!"

Kapot Guha shook his head and said, "We can't possibly have that kind of lionesses in a family-party like ours. Our society is not quite broad-minded enough to take it in its stride! Moreover, many of our literary giants are old men and therefore rather shy. They might feel awkward amidst lionesses. Now, if we could get hold of a literary lioness, it would be quite another matter. But they are rather difficult to find. When would you like to throw this party?;"

Sumanta and Sumitra said, " Let's have it on the day of Saraswati Puja. It will be great fun."

Kapot Guha said, "Oh no, we can't have it then. Most of the literary figures will have invitations to attend the puja at various places. But we might have the party two or three days later."

Becharam said, "Very well. January 25 happens to be a Sunday and should suit everyone. Whom do you intend to invite?"

"I'll discuss it with Shinjini and finalise the list. We don't really want a big crowd. Twenty-five to thirty people should be more than adequate. I'll tell you the names which I remember off hand. Bateswar Sikdar and Damodar Naskar, Galpa-Saraswati, are the most prominent literary lions of the present age, so we must have them both."

Sumitra said, "But it's common knowledge that the two just can't get on"

"That won't really matter. They can't come to blows at a party! And of course we must also ask Rajlaxmi Devi, Sahitya-Bhaswati. She is not quite a lioness but we can certainly call her a tigress. Then we must also have two traditional and two modern poets. Poets are not really much of an attraction, so four should be more than enough. We can ask Anukul Choudhury who is the editor of *Pragamini*, to preside over the function. And of course we should not leave out Kalachand Chongdar.

"Who on earth is he?" asked Sumanta.

"Don't you really know? He is the Editor of *Dundubhi*."

"But *Dundubhi* is supposed to be a rotten magazine." said Sumitra.

"Oh no, not at all. It has countless readers. The magazine believes in taking up a few select authors every week and tearing them to shreds. The readers gobble them up avidly."

"Doesn't it make the readers mad?"

"What on earth for? Every one enjoys reading gossip about famous people. In olden times the magazines which attacked Rabindranath Tagore attracted countless readers. Even the ardent admirers of the poet used to read them, laugh and say, "Ho, ho, ho! Just see what absurd things these chaps have come out with!" But this Kalachand Chongdar maintains certain principles. He doesn't touch small fry and spares all famous writers who make him a regular annual payment."

"Annual payment? Do you mean a kind of bribe?"

"Well, you could call it that. I've heard that Damodar Naskar pays Kalachand two hundred and fifty rupees during the pujas every year. It was Kalachand who was primarily responsible for his getting the title of *Galpa Saraswati*. Now, Bateswar Sikdar is an obstinate old miser and refuses to part with a paisa. As a result, he has to face a volley of abuse in every single issue of *Dhundubhi*. But I can't say that Kalachand never helps out people. Once three or four young chaps wrote a spate of obscene books which did not sell at all. So they went to Kalachand and said, "Please help us out, sir. Abuse our books violently in your magazine and quote choice passages from them. But unfortunately we cannot pay you more than fifty rupees. Please accept it". Kalachand agreed and the books were a complete sell-out"

"By the way, we must also ask Gorachand Sanpui, the editor of *Damama*, to our party. This chap does not exactly accept bribes but he takes money from rich authors and praises their trashy books to the skies in his magazine. Moreover, he makes it a point to abuse Kalachand in every issue. Anyway, I'll complete my list by tomorrow and finalise whom we should invite, what the menu should be, details of seating arrangements and everything."

The day of the much-talked-of party arrived. A shamiana was put up in the front lawn with small tables and chairs arranged in cosy groups. The guests were to have their tea here. A platform was put up at one end of the shamiana with seats for Anukul Choudhury who was to preside over the function, the two 'lions' Bateswar and Damodar plus a few special guests including Rajlaxmi Devi. There would not be any formal speech. Just Becharam welcoming the guests and Anukul telling the assembled group a few words about their generous host and thereby introducing him formally to everyone present. Of course, every one hoped that both Bateswar and Damodar would remember to say something complimentary about Becharam's abilities and generosity.

Three beautiful chairs had been specially procured for the president and the two chief guests - one made of Mysore sandalwood and the other two made of Kashmir walnut wood. The first chair had a high back and was elaborately carved. It looked far more ornamental than the other two. Kapot had tried his utmost to get hold of three identical chairs but could not manage it. He had also arranged for three violin players, belonging to the Charakdanga string band. They were to hide behind the shamiana and play softly from the background, so as not to disturb the guests.

The invited guests started arriving one by one. Becharam, his son and daughter, Kapot and Shinjini Guha greeted them cordially and found seats for them.

But Subala refused to be one of the party. She whispered a few polite words to Rajlaxmi Devi and sneaked out, after peeping inside the shamiana once or twice. Bateswar Sikdar and Damodar Naskar arrived last of all. By some strange coincidence both turned up exactly at the same time, each followed by a troupe of young and faithful fans. Becharam and Kapot welcomed both the parties most respectfully and escorted the highly esteemed lions within the shamiana.

Anukul Choudhury, the president, had arrived already. He sat down on one of the walnut chairs. Bateswar was older by age, so Kapot requested him to take the sandal wood chair. Sumitra placed a thick garland of tuberoses round his neck. Kapot requested Damodar to take the other chair made of walnut wood. But Damodar refused to sit down and continued to stand, holding his head high. Kapot made his request once again, "Kindly sit down, Sir." Damodar frowned and said, " I can't possibly sit on that chair!"

The shamiana soon rang with the hum of hushed whispers. Many of the guests stood up and walked up to the two lions. Kalachand Chongdar, the editor of *Dundubhi* said," Mr. Damodar can never sit on this inferior chair. It would be most insulting - since he happens to be the unrivalled king of Bengali literature! I am not criticizing Mr. Bateswar, but we demand that he give up his superior chair to Mr. Damodar who is more deserving." Gourchand Sanpui, the editor of *Damama* cried, "Don't you dare stir a step, Mr. Bateswar. Sit tight where you are. You are the king of Bengali literature - not Mr. Damodar!"

Kalachand said, "Nonsense ! Don't talk rubbish ! Mr. Damodar has a title - *GalpaSaraswati* What on earth does Mr. Bateswar have ? A big nought!"

Gaur Chand said, "Is that all ? I say, Bhupesh,

Rajen, Abani, Nuruddin and Nabakesto - come here, quick! There are six of us here — an editor, a short-story-writer, a long-story-writer, a writer of articles, a critic and a poet. We six, on behalf of all literary men of Bengal, hereby confer the title of 'Unrivalled Fiction King' *(Apratidwandi Galpa-Shilpa-Samrat)* to Mr. Bateswar Sikdar, on this day of -,year -, at - hours. Anyone who dares to protest, can challenge me this instant. I don't have gloves on me at the moment, but I proclaim my challenge by taking off my left socks. My challenger can pick it up now. I am game for anything - punching, slapping, clubs or brick bat, whatever you say."

No one came forward to pick up the socks. Gaur Chand said, "Nuru dear, blow the conch-shell loud and strong." Nuruddin put his hand to his mouth and made the sound of blowing a conch-shell.

Kalachand shouted, "Mr. Bateswar, if you care about your own good, you'd better vacate the chair instantly. What! You won't? Very well! Mr. Damodar, why are you standing still? Come and occupy the seat that is rightfully yours. You too sit down on the same chair."

Damodar said, "But there isn't any space for me to sit !" Kalachand and two of his cronies caught hold of Damodar and put him on Bateswar's lap, saying, "Don't you dare get up! We are here to back you up! Let's see how long old Bateswar can stand your eighty-kilo-bulk!"

A regular hullabaloo broke out. Sahitya-Bhaswati Rajlaxmi said, "Shame on you! Quarrelling like kids ! Aren't you ashamed of yourselves ? Get down from the chair, both of you, and let's all go and sit down at the tea table." Kalachand said, "Don't you listen to anybody Mr. Damodar. Just sit tight on Bateswar's lap."

Gaur Chand said, "Mr. Bateswar, push off Damodar from your chair. Pinch him, tickle him - do anything to throw him off. "

The assembled guests promptly split up into two groups - one supporting Bateswar, the other shouting in favour of Damodar. The two opposing parties nearly came to blows. Anukul Choudhury tried his best to plead and quieten them. But it was of no use. His efforts went in vain. Kapot Guha whispered to Becharam, "Doesn't look too good! Let's call in the police, shall we?"

Sumanta said, "Oh no. Let's call the Fire Brigade instead. A stiff stream of water from their hose pipes will cool both lions and the assembled jackals most effectively!"

Sumitra said, "We can't do either. It will merely cause a nasty scandal. I'll arrange to put an end to all this." And she left the place and rushed out of the gate at lightning speed.

There was an empty field right next to Becharam's house where the members of the local 'Jai Hind Club' were celebrating Saraswati puja. Although the main puja was over three days ago, the celebrations still continued. The image of the Goddess had not been immersed as yet. The members were busy making their final arrangements. The image had been brought down from the platform. The loud speaker lay on the floor but the wires had not been disconnected. It still continued to blare out hit music. A lorry stood in front, ready to take them away. A few boys and girls were ready with their masks. They were to dance before the Goddess in the lorry.

Becharam had contributed handsomely to the celebrations of the Jai Hind Club and had also helped them in various other ways. As a result, the boys of the club were particularly attentive to his entire family. Sumitra went straight to Prandhan Nag, who was the secretary of the club, and said, "Listen, we're in great trouble and I'll be very grateful if you come to our rescue."

"Tell us what we should do" cried Prandhan eagerly. "Just command, and it shall be done - to the best of our ability - whatever the task might be !"

Sumitra told him about the situation in brief and added that a few hooligans, who had also turned up at the party, meant to have a riot. The two lions, who were the chief guests, were sitting on the same chair and neither agreed to get up. Something nasty was bound to happen if someone did not move them immediately.

Prandhan said, "Very well. You needn't worry any more. I'll attend to your two lions before immersing our Godess. I'm sure mother Saraswati won't mind waiting an hour longer. You there - Bhuto, Beni, Matra and Hebo, come along with me ! Quick ! Niranjan Singh, get your lorry started. We'll be back right now."

Prandhan entered the shamiana with his four followers and said, "Here you are, Mr. Lions. Kindly vacate the chair you are sitting on. You don't wish to be the laughing-stalk of everyone, do you?"

Both Kalachand and Gaurchand cried out in a duet, "Don't you dare leave the chair !"

Prandhan said, "Indeed ! Here, Bhuto, Beni, Matra and Hebo, come forward, quick ! Mr. Lions, if you really wont get down from the chair, then you'd better hold on to the handles with all your might."

In a moment the followers of Prandhan picked up the chair, with both the lions clinging to its handles, and placed it right inside the lorry. Then they jumped inside and called to the driver, "Start now, Nirnajan Singh. Take us straight to the Alipore Zoo." The loud speaker was still blaring out , "Is it proper to stay so close together, my Love!"

The lorry stopped right in front of the zoo. Prandhan pushed out Bateswar and Damodar and said with folded hand, "Please don't take me amiss, dear Sirs. I've heard that both of you are famous people and that you've turned crazy because of two unmitigated hooligans. Well, it's all a question of destiny, you know, and you both are mere pawns. I suppose you couldn't help it. But don't worry. I've spoken to both your drivers. They'll be along to pick you up in half an hour's time. You both can indulge in a little tete-a-tete till then ! So long !"

All the assembled guests were somewhat thunderstruck at the unexpected consequence of the party. Kalachand and Gaurchand took themselves off unceremoniously. Many of the guests followed suit.

But the party wasn't an utter wash-out, after all. There were quite a few level-headed people, including Anukul Choudhury and Rajlaxmi Devi. They all stayed put. Every one expressed his heartfelt sympathies to Becharam, spoke strongly against Bateswar and Damodar's disgusting exhibition, and the villainy of Kalachand and Gaurchand. They expressed grave concern about the future of Bengali literature; ate a good many fish-patties, meat-chops, and a great deal of fried rice, cakes and sweets; drank umpteen cups of tea; thanked their host and bade a gracious farewell after promising to come again soon.

The Sheep-makers

It was a winter evening. A group of people sat on a durry spread out on the grassy river bank at the Botanical Gardens at Shibpur. The group consisted of Nikunja Ghosh, a senior professor, his wife Urmila and their fifteen-year-old daughter Ila. Suruchi, the wife of junior professor Biren Dutta, (who was the brother-in-law of professor Ghosh) and her six-year-old son, Nutu and old Sheetal Choudhury were there too. Sheetal was distantly related to Biren. Every one, young and old, called him "Uncle Sheetu."

Biren Dutta had not joined the party as yet. His friend Sukomal Gupta, newly wed, had just landed up from Assam with his wife and mother-in-law. Biren had gone there to escort the party to this picnic.

Sheetal Choudhury suddenly remarked - "What sort of a picnic is this, pray? There seems to be no edibles of any kind! Are we going to fill up our tummies with just fresh air?"

Suruchi said, "Don't worry, Uncle Sheetu, my husband has gone to fetch the lot - Major Sukomal, his wife, mother-in-law and loads of edibles! Mrs. Gupta and her mother have promised to cook everthing themselves. They owe us a feast anyway, as we couldn't go to their wedding. So they plan to make up for it this evening."

Nutu said, "Uncle Sheetu, you never completed the story which you started last eveing. Since there's no chance of our eating just yet, please complete the story now."

Uncle Sheetu said -"Very well. Here goes. The King married his second queen and brought her home amidst a great deal of fanfare, with bugles, drums, flutes, castanots and what-have-you, playing loud and strong. Fifty conch-shells blew simultaneously and all the aunts of the king cheered as loud as they could. The poor first queen felt terribly depressed and went off to her father's house with her little son. Now, the second queen happened to be a she-ogre. Before the week was done the king got the news of his horses and elephants dying in their stables with just their teeth, bones and tails lying on the floor!

"Couldn't the second queen chew those ?" asked Nutu curiously.

"Shut up" said Suruchi in a cross voice. "There's no need for you to relate such horrid stories, Uncle Sheetu. Why do you come out with these gruesome tales ? They have a very bad influence on young minds!"

Nikunja Ghosh laughed outright and said -"Oh no! It's not quite so bad ! You find such things in the fairy tales of every country - giants, ogres and all that. They don't harm the children. Children can understand that these stories are all made-up ones, not to be taken seriously. Isn't that so, Nutu?"

Nutu said, "Yes. I can make up stories too."

Suruchi said, "That may be so but, please don't tell him these horrible false stories, Uncle Sheetu."

Uncle Sheetu said, "Of course I shan't, since you object to it. Nutu, please ask your mother to tell you stories of Surpanakha. That's a lovely true story! And I think all of you ought to know one plain fact. You can't say that everything about a fairy-tale is necessarily false. Some of it is certainly based on actual facts."

Urmila, Nikunja's wife asked - "Tell me, Uncle Sheetu, do you really believe in Ogre-queens, princesses of the underworld, magic wands and females of Kamaksha who are supposed to turn men into sheep?"

"Of course, I believe in some of these things, specially about men turning into sheep."

Ila said -"But why do you believe in that particular story, Uncle Sheetu? Please tell us."

"How can I, when Nutu's mother objects to it so strongly?"

Nikunja Ghosh said, "But it's not fair to rouse a person's curiosity and then hold one's tongue. Far better to make a clean breast of everything." Suruchi said -"Oh very well. You'd better tell us the story of the sheep. But please leave out the lurid details"."I'd rather not," said Uncle Sheetu, "speak of sheeps, I mean. Let's talk about God and divinity instead. Ila dear, why don't you sing a Rabindrasangeet for us ? Sing that one about bowing my head low beneath the dust of Thy feet."

Suruchi said, "Uncle Sheetu, don't put on the martyr-act, for goodness' sake ! I beg your pardon for having said anything. Do tell us the sheep story." Nutu said, "No, Uncle Sheetu, let's hear about the ogre-queen first."

"Shut up, Baby," said Suruchi, "the story of sheep is better than the story of ogres, any day. Please begin, Uncle Sheetu". So, Sheetal Choudhury started his tale.

"It all happened twenty five years ago. Probably none of you are familiar with the name of Balabhadra Mardaraj. Balabhadra's father Ramabhadra was a famous Zamindar in the Baleswar district. He was nearly as important as a king. I used to work in his estate in those days. Balabhadra was around thirty, good looking, good tempered and really keen on hunting. He told me one day, "Well Sheetal, you'll really go crazy one of these days if you do nothing but keep accounts. I'll speak to father about it and get him to sanction you twenty days' leave. You can come along with me to Keemapur. It is in the north east of Assam, a really wonderful place for hunting. You even get the eighteen-lumped deer over there. They are not very big in size but have a couple of really weird horns - each one has nine lumps on it."

Balabhadra was to pay for it all. As I'd merely have to accompany him and play the perfect yes-man, I agreed to his proposal at once. Keemapur was a rather out-of-the-way place, right on the other side of the Brahmaputra. It was actually on the Bhutan border, in spite of being a part of the Kamrup district. The road was pretty bad. The car just about managed to make it. Balabhadra had the reputation of being a good Shikari so it was fairly easy to get all the necessary permits from the Assam Government. We landed up at the Keemapur dak bungalow in a huge Hudson car. We had a driver, a servant and loads of edibles with us. We went out hunting every day and managed to shoot all kinds of animals. But there was no trace of the special deer we were looking for. The local people told us that they lived further up north, right at the heart of the dense forest. The car could go just a fraction of the way and we'd have to walk the rest.

We started at about 8 a.m. the next day. There were four of us in the car - Balabhadra, Kirpan Singh, our driver, a Bhutia who was to show us the way and myself. The road was really terrible. The car tyre was punctured twice. It took us full three hours to go just three miles. It was 11 a.m. and blazing hot. We were famished and looked eagerly for a suitable place to rest awhile. Just then we spotted a pretty little cottage hidden among the trees. As we walked towards it, an exceedingly pretty girl stepped out of the cottage. She was very fair and had a ravishing figure, although her nose was somewhat flat and she also had slit eyes. We greeted her and told her who we were. The beauty informed us that her name was Mayavati Kurunji and that she was quite alone at the moment, as her aunt, who lived with her, had gone for marketing at Keemapur accompanied by their servant. Mayavati spoke to us in pure Bengali, although her words had an Assamese twang. She invited us in quite cordially and we accepted her invitation gracefully.

It was quite apparent from Balabhadra Mardaraj's behaviour that he had fallen madly in love with Mayavati at first sight. His soppy, melting tone as he spoke to her, made it more than obvious. Laden Gampa, our Bhutia Guide, ambled up to me quietly and whispered - "That lady is a dangerous one. Run away from this place immediately." But we hardly listened to him. Balabhadra was already fathoms deep in love and I too was rather fascinated by her charms.

Mayavati was most attentive to us both. She told us that this was not the season for the eighteen-lumped deer and that they came down from the hills only during the winter months. If we turned up again in two month's time, we were sure to come across them. We promised to come back, thanked her profusely and bade adieu.

We shot a few birds on our way back and returned to the Dak Bungalow at Keemapur. Balabhadra went to see Mayavati again the next day. I stayed back at the bungalow as I didn't feel too well. Balabhadra returned late that evening and said - "Listen to me, Sheetal. I intend to marry Miss Mayavati and take her to Calcutta with me in fifteen days' time. You'd better go there tomorrow itself, fix up a good house for us at Ballygunge and await our coming. I tried my level best to convince him that it was not the done thing to marry a complete stranger so suddenly and that his father wouldn't put up with it either. But Balabhadra turned a deaf ear to all my words. So there was nothing I could do but start for Calcutta the very next day.

Balabhadra's driver Kirpan Singh came to me after a fortnight and informed me that Balabhadra was missing. No one had the foggiest notion as to where he was. Even Mayavati could tell them nothing about his whereabouts. After a great deal of cross-examination I learnt that the car had been out of order four days ago and Balabhadra had walked over to Mayavati's place. When his master failed to turn up that evening, Kirpan himself went there to make enquiries. But when he turned up, there was only Mayavati and her old aunt in the house. They admitted that Balabhadra had come to see them in the morning but they had absolutely no idea as to where he was at the moment or where he went after leaving their house. Kirpan Singh also noticed a well-grown and healthy brown sheep tied to a pole on the varanda, chewing grams placidly.

Suruchi cried, "Uncle Sheetu, are you trying to imply that the sheep was Balabhadra?"

"I am implying nothing. I am just telling you exactly what I'd been told. It's up to you to draw conclusions - to believe, or to disbelieve!"

Nutu asked, "Uncle Sheetu, why was the sheep eating grams? Wasn't there any grass in that place?"

Ila said, "Don't you understand, Baby? The lady

was preparing gram-fed-mutton! Oh dear! You really had a narrow shave, Uncle Sheetu!"

Just then Biren Dutta, Suruchi's husband, reached there with two ladies. Two servants followed them, carrying huge baskets of food. One of the ladies looked around fifty. The other one was in her early twenties. Both were extraordinarily beautiful, although they had the typically Mongolian touch about the eyes and nose.

Biren Dutta introduced them both. "Meet Mrs. Mayavati Mardaraj", the mother-in-law of Sukomal Gupta. This is Mrs. Mohini Gupta, Sukomal's wife. Sorry we got a little delayed. The ladies were busy cooking a variety of dishes, you see."

Ila whispered -'Uncle Sheetu, is this the same Mayavati you were telling us about ?'

"Shut up, she 'll hear you" said Sheetal, hushing her up.

Nikunja Ghosh said - "Where's major Gupta ? Hasn't he come too"

"Sukomal?" said Mohini in a honeyed voice, "Don't talk of the poor fellow. Can't think where he has vanished all of a sudden !"

'Good gracious !' Cried Ila with a shudder. Mayavati said "The army can be quite awful that way. He had an unexpected call and just dashed off without informing anybody ! Please start eating, all of you, or the food will go cold. Mohini and I shall serve you."

Biren Dutta said - 'Uncle Sheetu, you can eat everything quite unhesitatingly. They know that you don't take chicken. So they've made every single thing - cutlets, fries, pies, chops and kababs - with pure mutton. Anyway, the ladies are from Kamrup, Assam, so sheep happens to be their specialitily!' And Biren guffawed loudly at his own joke.

"Oh Good God!" Cried Ila in a choking voice. "Won't you ladies join us too?" asked Nikunja.

'Oh no. We've just had a meal' said Mayavati smiling. Ila stood up with a shudder and cried - "Oh oh ... oh heaven help me !"

Suruchi jumped up and said - "I feel sick ! I'd better go and sit by the Ganges !"

Urmila said "I'll join you. I too am feeling rather queer all of a sudden!"

Ila rushed after them. Biren followed them anxiously and said - "Mrs. Gupta has also brought six bottles of soda with her. Why not have some ? You'll soon feel better then." Suruchi cried -"Not on my life! I refuse to touch anything made by those wretched females."

When Biren heard the whole story after coming home he said, "Good gracious ! How could you possible be so silly and gullible ? No wonder the scriptures maintain that female-learning is a dangerous thing! How on earth could you believe uncle Sheetu's cock-and-bull story ? Didn't you see how he positively gorged himself with all that food?"

The Reincarnation of Kashinath

All this happened nearly a couple of centuries ago. It was the time when the Bengali community of Calcutta was just beginning to undergo a variety of changes. But the villages were, as yet, quite unaware of them. So was also the case with the village of Raghavpur. Kashinath Sarvabhauma, the undisputed head of the village, was a reputed scholar and known for his practical sense. His children and grandchildren had scattered far and wide, taking up residence in Calcutta, Hooghly, Burdwan, Krishnagar, Murshidabad and other places. But nothing could induce Kashinath to leave his native village. Not only did he live there and run his own zamindari but also ran a successful pawning business and a Sanskrit school. He also looked after the temple and all rituals connected with it.

Kashinath had a strange dream one night. At almost daybreak, one might say. He dreamt that the Goddess Kali was standing right before him. "Dear Kashinath" said the Goddess, "you have lived more than a hundred years, enjoying life to the full. Why linger on indefinitely ? Better start thinking of life hereafter and get prepared for death."

"Sorry, Divine Mother" said Kashinath, "But I'm afraid I can't oblige you at the moment! I really can't die now ! Why, my fourth wife is still alive and so are my eighteen children. I still have a hundred and twenty-five grandchildren. I must have had more than a thousand great-grand-children - though many of them have passed away. But I dare say a sizable number is still alive ! Moreover, I have several students who study in my school. I teach them and look after them. The very thought of leaving all these dear ones behind is an extremely painful one. I have made up my mind to dedicate a huge temple to you, so I have to get it built as well. In case the ill winds of modern fashion enter my village, it is I who must put a stop to it ! I know that my sons are going to do nothing about it. They are all selfish and much too wrapped up in their own affairs. I know that I am getting on in years, but I am pretty fit yet. So, please let me live for another ten years at least."

Goddess Kali frowned and disappeared from the scene. When Kashinath awoke the next morning, Raseswari, his fourth wife, reminded him that he had a lot of things to do. "Don't forget that you have to perform the rice- ceremony for eight of your great-grand-children this morning. I don't suppose you remembered it ? Better go and finish your morning ablutions because it is you who have to perform the yajna."

Kashinath hurried towards the Ganges for his usual dip. As he came home after his bath, there was a grim shadow on his face. "I'm undone, Wife !"he cried in a pathetic voice, "I've been fatally bitten by a snake. I know that my last moment has arrived. What am I to do, Mother Goddess ? What have you done ? Why send me to the land of death before I have completed all that I meant to do ?"

The scriptures tell us that each one of us gets his desserts in accordance with one's convictions before death. Had Kashinath fallen a victim to the missionaries of Serampore and become a Christian, he would have had to wait a long, long while for the final day of Judgement. Rather like the way reptiles hibernate during the winter. But luckily for him, Kashinath happened to be a devout Hindu so his fate was decided pretty fast.

Kashinath felt his spirit flitting about in space while his lifeless body lay still before the tulasi grove. He saw his wife and relatives mourning his death. He heard his neighbours say that it was a major catastrophe. Soon afterwards his spirit soared upwards at break neck speed and he found himself before Yamaraj, the God of death.

"Welcome, Kashinath" said Yama, "I have already made a complete assessment of your good and bad deeds on earth and have also chalked out what exactly you are to do. Let me sum it up for your benefit. Your bad deeds are quite negligible compared to your good ones. You had wrongly grabbed part of Ramgati Bhattacharya's property. You had given false witness thrice in court. You cast lewd glances towards several of your friends' wives and also at girls young enough to be your daughters. You had produced countless brats with the abandon of a thoughtless tom cat and had been deeply steeped in worldly desires right upto your last moment. Apart from these, all that you have done are mainly good deeds. You have worshipped the Goddess faithfully for all these years. You took regular dips in the Ganges, went on pilgrimage, observed every religious ritual and did all that a conscientious Brahmin ought to do. You have never eaten any forbidden food. That's the list, in short. You have to live in hell for fifty years to atone for your sins. After that you shall live in heaven for a hundred years as a result of your good deeds. Go and begin at once."

Kashinath spent the stipulated period in hell and heaven and was called back to face Yama once again.

"Well Kashinath" said Yama, "You have paid for your good and bad deeds. Which means, you have to go back to earth once again. God is quite pleased with you. So He says you can choose where exactly you wish to be reborn. Please tell me what you'd like. Would you like to be the son of a rich merchant or that of a poor but wise and saintly man ? Or would you rather be born in a pure and devout home ?

"Well, Dharmaraj, I happened to have a number of unfulfilled desires when I died" said Kashinath, "So please send me back to a living member of my own family. Bhabani Charan, the son of my great-grandson was specially dear to me. Please let me be reborn as his son.'

"Really, Kashinath, you seem to be quite crazy !" said Yama "Don't you remember that you had seen five generations even when you were alive ? Full hundred and fifty years have passed since your death. Which means another six generations, at least ! The existing member of that family is barely related to you ! What on earth are you going to gain by being born there? Specially when there are so many better families around!"

"I don't care, my Lord, but do please send me to someone in Bhabani's family - however many generations removed he might be ! After all, he owes his origin to me and my dear Bhabani Charan ! I am bound to feel a great affection for him and I must admit that I am extremely eager to meet him !"

"But how on earth are you going to recognise him?" asked Yama in surprise, "It is not, as if you are going to retain your memory even after you are reborn ! You are going to be a tiny little infant at first, minus sense or memory. Of course you are going to learn everything once you grow up. But you will remember nothing about your past life then."

"Please listen to me, my Lord" said Kashinath, "I have no wish to remain a prisoner inside a woman's womb for nine months and be reborn as a wee infant. Please send me as a grown up young man who remembers everything."

"Well, you were well over a hundred at the time of death. Do you mean to say that you want to be born as an old man of that precise age?"

"Not quite, Sir. What is the point of my being reborn at all if I go down on earth as an old man? I want to enjoy my youth! Please let me go as a young man of thirty or so."

"Your desire is a wierd one!" grumbled Yama. "You dont wish to repose in a woman's womb and want to be reincarnated as a young man, with full memory of your past incarnation, in a family belonging to a relative of yours. Is that it?"

"Yes Sir, that's about it."

"Very well. Be it so. Let us see what happens and how the idea works. What is your gotra, by the way?"

"Bharadwaj, Sir."

Yama closed his eyes, sinking deep in meditation. Finally he said, "Look here, man, a lot of social changes have taken place on earth. Had you been reborn the traditional way, as a tiny little infant, you could have got used to the changes quite naturally. But your sudden appearance as a young man in a totally unfamiliar set-up will put you to any number of hassles. However, I shall try my level best to see that they are kept to a minimum."

Yama sent for one of his assistants. "This man here shall return to the earth tonight, exactly at midnight.

He will be reincarnated as a young man of thirty." said Yama pointing to Kashinath. "So you'd better teach him the modern dialect spoken in West Bengal at the moment. Let him also pick up a smattering of English and Hindi (the kind spoken in Bengal, of course !). Give him adequate clothes and other necessary things required by modern people and plenty of money. Also an "Expulsion" tablet, which will enable him to return here instantly, in case he cannot stand it. Carry him to Calcutta and leave him in front of the gate of house number three on Sri Madhusudan Road. Asleep, of course." Turning to Kashinath he added, "Look here, Kashinath, I am sending you down to your relative's place. He is called Chakradhar Mukherjee. You may retain your old name. In case you find the present kind of society too painful and feel that you can't adjust to it, then you may swallow the expulsion tablet. It will bring you back to my abode. You will then be sent off to be reborn the traditional way."

Chakradhar Muhkerjee, the Managing Director of a City Corporation, was a wealthy man. His residence on 3. Sri Madhusudan Road was quite a palatial one. As a rule he never left his bed before eight in the morning. But this morning his wife Surupa shook him vigorously at the crack of dawn. "What's up ?"asked Chakradhar is surprise.

"Can't you hear the hullaballoo downstairs. Go to the balcony and ask them what the matter is" said Surupa, "I feel rather scared."

Chakradhar looked down from the balcony and saw a crowd in front of his gate, all talking nineteen to the dozen. "What's up, Lal Bahadur ?"he asked the durwan.

"There is a man here, lying in front of the gate"said Lal Bahadur, "we can't make out if he is alive or dead."

Chakradar came downstairs and walked up to the gate. He saw a stranger, lying unconsious, a leather bag under his head. Chakradar shook him briskly. The man opened his eyes, yawned, blinked and sat up.

"Goddess Kali," he muttered to himself, "Where have you brought me, Mother ?"

"Who are you ?"asked Chakradhar sternly, "Do you still feel tipsy ? And what did you take? Liquor ? Or was it hash ?"

"I am Sri Kashinath Mukhopadhyay, the great scholar, reincarnated once more" said Kashinath. Are you Chakradhar ? The great-great-great-great grandson of my dear Bhabani Charan ? Dear me, how you've grown ! you're quite a man ! Let us go in, my dear, and I shall tell you everything."

Chakradhar felt convinced that the man was not drunk. Nor did he sound like a drug-addict. He did not seem to be a crook or a theif either. But he was positively mad ! There was no doubt about it.

"What are you carrying in that bag of yours ?"asked Chakradhar.

"No idea"said Kashinath. "Why don't you open it and see ? I have a key here, tied to my sacred thread. Here, take it."

Chakradhar opened the bag. It contained a few dhotis and kurtas, vests, underclothes, a scarf, a pair of slippers, a comb and mirror, etc. There was a portfolio at the bottom of the bag. Chakradhar was struck dumb with surprise when he opened it. It contained Government papers worth five lakhs, some excellent company shares, around two thousand rupees in cash and a big bundle of change in coins.

"All the papers and shares are in your name !" cried

Chakradhar in surprise. "How on earth did you manage to acquire so much ?"

"I know nothing, my dear. It is all the doings of the Divine Mother and Yamaraj. They must have given it to me" said Kashinath.

Chakradhar thought deeply for sometime. The man might be quite mad but he didnt quite sound like one. In any case, a wealthy man like him should not be allowed to slip off his hands. Chakradhar made up his mind to detain Kashinath in his own house and get him treated by a psychiatrist. He was quite young, after all. Barely thirty, if that much. It was a pity that his only daughter was married already. But his niece Chandana was not. If only he could manage Kashinath, the poor orphan girl's life would be made. Investments worth five lakhs was no joke. And certainly not an amount to be sneezed at ! If only the fellow had truned up three years earlier Chakradhar would certainly have married him to his own daughter.

"Look here, Kashinath" he said, "You may be my forefather, as you say, but right now you happen to be much younger than I am. I don't think you are more than thirty whereas I am sixty. I may believe in your queer history but don't mention it to another soul. They'll think that you're plain batty ! Just tell them that you are distantly related to me. Say that you had run away with a hermit in your childhood while you were living in the village. Now that you are fed up of living a saintly life, you have come back to me. You must also address me as "Uncle" and I shall call you "Kashi". And don't you breathe a word about your property to anyone else, do you hear me ?"

"Yes, I understand", said Kasinath, "But I don't see how I can possibly live in your house. I, find that you have already turned outlandishly unconventional ! I can see chicks romping in your garden and I can actually smell onions. Shocking! And I saw a middle aged dame walk downstairs with slippers on. Her head was uncovered and she looked me straight in the eyes !"

"Oh that would be my wife, your aunt."

"Indeed ! But how dare a woman wear slippers ! Damn the modern age !"

"You may curse it all you like but this is the age you have to live in, my dear !"

"I suppose you also eat stuff made by a Muslim cook, eh ? Well, I cant ! Not in a million years !"

"Not quite. My cook is a Harijan. Probably his folks were shoe-makers."

"Lord save, me ! I shall cook myself. I shall have just fruits and milk today. Please arrange for a separate establishment for me."

"Very well. You can live in the eastern wing of my house. It's quite private. "Then Chakradhar called out to his niece. "Chandana, where are you ? Come here, will you, dear ?"

A young girl walked into the room. "Meet my niece", said Chakradhar, "Chandana, this is your cousin Kashi. Touch his feet." Chandana greeted him the traditional way and left the room. Kashinath stood staring for a while and finally said - "I don't understand what you're up to ! Why doesn't the girl have vermillion on her forehead ? Dont tell me she is a widow !"

"Certainly not ! She is not even married. She is a very bright girl and has just done her graduation."

"Goodness gracious ! Such a huge big girl and not yet married ! Are you quite crazy ?"

"Now Kashinath, surely you intend to get married?"

"Of course I do. You'd better send for a good match-maker."

"Why don't you marry my niece Chandna?"

"Are you quite off your head, Chakradhar? Marry a girl belonging to the same family ? Moreover, such a hoity-toity won't suit me at all ! I want a shy, reserved, conservative girl belonging to a good family. She need not be educated. It will do if she knows how to cook and other household chores. She should be able to observe every religious ritual. I dont want an upstart like that wife and niece of yours."

"Now you're putting me in a soup, Kashinath ! The brand of girls like the one you're asking for just don't exist nowadays ! At least not in educated families ! Anyway, I shall see what I can do. Go and have your bath now. Eat something and rest a while."

Chakradhar Mukherjee thought long and deep about the whole situation. The man seemed crazy no doubt, but his words were not inconsistent. In spite of being hopelessly old fashioned he seemed to be a pretty shrewd customer ! What was most surprising was his having all that money. Where on earth could he have grabbed it from ? Anyway, one thing was obvious. He just had to detain the man anyhow and keep a firm hold on his property. It would have been just wonderful if he could get him to agree to marry Chandana. He would be absolutely in his pocket, in that case. Now, finding a girl of his choice might prove to be a tough job. It had to be an old fashioned girl who would be able to keep such a nutty husband in leash, and be in Chakradhar's control at the same time ! Not an easy proposition, by a long chalk !

A sudden brainwave struck him just then. What about Gayeshwari ? She would make him an excellent bride ! Gayeshwari was tremendously old fashioned and conservative, was frightfully touchy about what was proper and ritualistic and what's more, she thought a lot of *his* opinion on all matters. She might very well agree to marry Kashinath because of his money. But there was a great difference in their ages ! Far too much, in fact !

Gayeshwari was a distant niece of Chakradhar. Her mother was his first cousin. Gayeshwari was as yet unmarried inspite of having turned fifty. She lost her parents at a young age so Chakradhar had been her guardian at first. But he didn't really have to look after her for long. Gayeshwari was quite an extraordinary woman. She managed to become independent after a little education by learning some arts and crafts. Now she ran a most successful shop managed exclusively by females and made heavy profits. Five refugee girls and two tailors worked in her shop. The three sewing machines ran nonstop and the shop was perpetually chockful of customers. Chakradhar had often tried to get Gayeshwari married. But she always pooh poohed the idea. "Nothing doing !" she told him firmly, "I've built up my business with great pain and I just wont have a strange fellow barging in and bossing over us all !" Chakradhar decided to go about the business with utmost caution and broach the subject very delicately to both Kashinath and Gayeshwari.

Fortunately for all, Kashinath and Gayeshwari met by chance just after Chakradhar thought of the idea.

Kashinath had set up his separate establishment in the eastern wing of Chakradhar's house. He did his own cooking. One of Chakradhar's servants ran errands for him. One morning Kashinath was shopping in the Gariahat market. The place was unusually crowded on account of its being the day of *Jamai-shasti*. Kashinath was terribly annoyed at the price of things. A seer of brinjal for twelve annas! Why, it was day light robbery! Why on earth were the things so outrageously expensive? Was there a famine or something? Kashinath wanted to buy a couple of green bananas and was proceeding carefully towards the banana stall, bag in hand, when he had a head-on collision with Gayeshwari.

Actually it was not Kashinath's fault at all. He was a short and thin man and had been knocked forward by the pushing crowd. Just then Gayeshwari was coming from the opposite direction. She was a veritable walking mountain against whom Kashinath's mini form had stood still. Gayeshwari was not shaken by the bump. But she was extremely annoyed.

"Are you drunk stupid fellow ? Toppling on top of a lady like this ! How dare you ?"

"Forgive me, Madam" said Kashinath in a repentant voice, "I didn't do it deliberately. I fell on you because people pushed me from the back."

"Of course you did it deliberately, you shameless scoundrel !" cried Gayeshwari "You are hundred per cent guilty !"

Almost immediately a proper fight broke out - one group supporting Gayeshwari and the other group supporting Kashinath. Most people knew Gayeshwari already. A young priest said - "Dear me, Gayadidi, you have to perform penance, you know. Being clasped by a young man is no small matter !"

Four or five others shouted - "Yes, of course you must !"

"You, fellow, where are you from ?" they asked Kashinath, "Must be from some remote rustic village ! You should have known better than to fall on top of a formidable person like Gayeshwari ! You'd better hand over fifty rupees - the cost of performing penance - or you've had it !"

Just then a servant of Chakradhar turned up and managed to save Kashinath. The priest finally said - "Oh very well, if both these people - Gayadidi and Kashinath - are relatives of Chakradhar, then I suppose he is the best person to settle the matter."

Chakradhar Mukherjee believed in striking the iron while it was hot. So he lost no time in suggesting his proposal to his niece.

"Are you off your head, Uncle?" cried Gayeshwari in amazement, "I never heard of anything so prepostrous in my life!" "The man might be a trifle batty but he is a good sort" assured Chakradhar, "You will find it perfectly easy to tame him. Don't forget that he has loads of money. What does it matter if he is a little younger than you are? Nobody minds such things nowadays."

Gayeshwari was a wily woman and saw the wisdom of her uncle's words. Finally she said, "Very well. I don't mind if the fellow agrees to the proposal. I don't really care what people say."

But Kashinath was a tougher nut to crack. "Don't speak like a lunatic, uncle Chakradhar" he told him, "Gayeshwari is nearly double my age. I know that the Kulin Brahmin girls in the last century married at her age. But I am not a professional groom!"

"Oh well, have it your way!" said Chakradhar with a shrug, "But I would advise you to consider the proposal from every angle. She is really a most devout person and observes every single ritual under the sun - including Amra-sasti. She may run a tailer's shop but she is every bit as old fashioned as you are! Once you marry her, you will be in charge of her shop. Which means a substantial increase in your income."

"But there is a vast difference in our ages!"

The Reincarnation of Kashinath

"So what ? If what you told me is really true, then you are well over two hundred and fifty years of age whereas poor Gayeshwari is only forty-nine. She is a babe compared to you, when it comes to actual age, that is! And consider another point. Your body might be young but your mind is more than two centuries old! I am sure you both will see eye to eye in every matter! There is something else as well. According to most scholars, women actually come of age after the age of fifty! Have you ever tasted a *"martaman"* banana? Mere ripening does not bring about perfect taste. When the skin darkens and shrivels a little and the pulp gets totally soft - it's that over-ripe fruit which actually tastes like nectar! Women are also like bananas! Sweet sixteen is not a patch on sweet fifty!"

Chakradhar's pleadings had the desired effect on Kashinath. He relented by degrees. He thought deeply for a while and said - "Now that I think of it, I remember that my fourth wife Raseswari must also have been Gayeswari's age when I passed away. It now seems as if Raseswari has been reincarnated as Gayeshwari. Well, you may ask the match-maker to proceed."

"I am the match-maker, and I have already spoken to Gayeshwari. She is willing , if you are. So you two can get married as soon as you have had a formal engagement. Why don't you go to her place this evening and have a talk with her ?"

"If I do, you must also be present, uncle Chakra."

"No, no, that's not the done thing these days ! Two's company, three's a crowd !"

Gayeshwari gave Kashinath a broad smile. "So, young man, do you like me ?" Kashinath nodded in silence.

"I hear you possess five lakh rupees ? Now, just listen to me. You must hand it all over to me the moment we are married. See ? You are such a nincompoop ! I can't possibly trust you with money. People are bound to cheat you and grab it all. In fact, I don't even trust that uncle of mine !"

"Don't worry, Madam Gayeshwari" said Kashinath, "The man who can cheat me is yet to be born ! I'll tell you what I've planned. I don't approve of women running shops. So I plan to sell it the moment we are married. I shall use the money - plus what I have - to set up a broker's business. Uncle Chakra tells me that one can no longer buy a zamindari these days. But you don't need to worry your head about these things. I shall get you all the jewellery you want and anything else that you may like to have. This Calcutta is a rotten place - fit for the devil alone. We are going to set up house in the village of Raghavpur. We shall have a house, a garden, a pond and a huge cow-shed. Of course, we must have a temple and a school as well."

Gayeshwari waved her arms in exasperation, saying, "I like that, you fool ! What a crazy notion ! Talk of raving lunatics ! You are one alright ! Listen to me, young fellow ! I may be your wife, but I am older than you are. So I am to be respected, see ? You are going to remain in my custody and do just as I tell you."

Kashinath was struck dumb for awhile. Then he muttered "Goddess Kali, save me" under his breath and left the place.

That evening after Kashinath was through with his nightly prayers, he addressed his complaints to the Goddess : "What sort of a situation have you landed me in Mother ?" he said aloud, "Not that I can blame you wholly ! I am being paid for my own folly ! I had never really imagined that the world has gone to the dogs like this! I find Muslim cooks in the house of Brahmins and chicken running all over the place! Old women strut about wearing shoes and huge big, grown up girls actually go to schools ! Lower castes have become most impertinent and don't revere Brahmins any more. They smoke quite openly before us ! I am going to be totally ruined in this place ! And that wretched Gayeshwari is an obnoxious female ! Marrying her would be no different from roasting eternally in hell ! Chakradhar is a perfect scoundrel. He can't possibly belong to my family. I am positive that Yamaraj has sent me to his place by mistake. Mother Kali, my Goddess, please tell me what I should do - and how I can save myself from my folly !"

Kashinath had a dream at dawn. He dreamt that the Goddess had appeared before him, saying "Get lost, Kashinath." He then realised that it had been very foolish on his part to come back to the earth in this manner. He made up his mind and swallowed the *Expulsion Tablet* Yama had given him. Immediately he was back in Yama's land once again.

The doctor examined Kashinath's body the next day and said "Thrombosis ! People don't usually have it at this age - unless they are lunatics."

Chakradhar tried to take his keys which always remained tied to Kashinath's sacred thread. But it was not there ! Then he tried to grab his portfolio but that too seemed to have disappeared mysteriously ! He dashed off to Gayeshwari's place, quite certain that she had got hold of it. Both had a battle royale over the missing portfolio but it was not to be found ! As a matter of fact, Yama's treasures had gone back to his treasury once again !

The Heavenly Slippers

Abukar Miya, a tailor residing in Hatibagan and his wife, Ramzani Bibi, were looking at the "Eid" moon which had just made its appearance in the western sky that evening. Ramzani suddenly noticed a strange object. She called out to her husband. "Look, dear, what is that strange sicklelike thing glittering right in the middle of the sky ?" Abukar stared at the sky for a long time and said - "Well, it's not quite like a sickle. Looks more like a 'Taltala' slipper to me. I rather think it's a gas balloon let off by the Mullicks."

Abukar's surmise was not quite correct because the same object was seen in the sky the very next evening and several evenings after that. It neither floated about like a gas balloon nor did it stay quite still and static. It set and rose like the sun and the moon. When people consulted Tarak Sanyal, the budding astrologer, he told them, "It looks like Neptune to me. Which means grave danger." Sasadhar Acharya, the senoir and best known amongst star-gazers, guffawed when he heard it and said, "Tarak's an arrant fool. Neptune resembles a human head whereas this object looks more like a tail. Which means it must be Pluto. It means grave disaster. You should all perform a yajna to pacify the planet and organise a nonstop, day-long chanting of God's name."

A regular panic spread all over the place. Newspapers reported various opinions and comments about the strange phenomenon. One of the reporters said, "Probably it is the flying saucer, looking somewhat flat and slipper-like on account of its having knocked against some star or the other." Another reporter said, "We feel sure that it is a tail-less comet. It is bound to acquire a fresh tail the moment it comes a little closer to the sun. The tail will then knock against our earth and bash it up. "Mr. Kunja Behari Talapatra, the elderly head of the Sanskrit department, wrote, "To which sage does this terrible and terrifying sky-slipper belong ? It resembles the wooden slippers of Ishwar Chandra Vidyasagar more than anything else ! Most probably the indignant soul of the departed scholar is livid at the stark irresponsibility of our so called educationists and has thrown down one of his slippers across the sky in sheer disgust ! The flying slipper is soon going to land upon their heads !"

Mr. Birupaksha Mandal, an important member of the opposite group, wrote, "Of course the slipper can't possibly belong to Sri Vidyasagar. None of his slippers ever had such a long and tapering snout ! I feel that the slipper belongs to our noble and deceased doctor, Sri Mahendra Lal Sarkar. He must be hopping mad about the various scandals currently raging in the Medical Colleges and hospitals ! Being bereft of surgical instruments in heaven, he has thrown down one of his slippers in angry protest. So, those in authority in the Medical Colleges, BEWARE !" Sri Hemanta Chattaraj, the devotional poet, wrote - "This sky-slipper does not belong to any human being at all ! It is a symbol of Divine fury. Lord Siva, the Nataraja, is enraged after seeing all the theft, bribery, adulteration, falsehood, hypocrisy and lechery prevalant upon this earth. So He raised His right foot to perform His famous "Dance of destruction," and the slipper slipped off His feet and toppled across the sky. His Dance is about to begin. Which means the end of the world. If all the men, women and children on earth do not come back to the path of virtue - *pronto* - the Divine anger is bound to consume the entire universe !"

Needless to say, the educated folk were not particularly impressed by any of these theories put across by laymen. They wanted to know what the specialists made of the phenomenon. Mr. Bishwambhar Chakrabarty, the proud owner of the Bishwambhar Cotton Mills, Bishwambhar Bank and the *Bishwambhar Chronicle* called himself a specialist-of- all-things and had never so far said "I don't know" to any query. But he too shook his head up and down with a grave expression when asked about the heavenly-slipper. People went round putting the same question to a select group of professors. All of them said - "It is difficult to say just what the object is. But it certainly cannot be a star because its axis is not parallel to any of the poles. This heavenly body might well be a planet, though. It could also be a comet minus tail. The terror caused by its appearance is perfectly legitimate. However small it might appear to the naked eye, the thing must actually be enormous in size. Let us see what the Kodaikanal Observatory reports about it. And the *Greenwich Report* too, of course."

Both reports arrived before long. All famous observatories here and abroad said more or less the same thing. Leaving aside the scientific details, what the reports roughly boiled down to was as follows : "The planet nearest to the sun is Mercury. Next comes Venus and then our Earth, followed by Mars, Jupiter, Saturn, Uranus, Neptune and Pluto. There is a huge constellation of asteroids between the axes of Mars and Jupiter, also revolving round the sun. One such asteroid has suddenly fallen out of its usual orbit and come close to earth. The asteroid in question is not round in shape so the Indian astronomers have named it the 'Heavenly Slipper'. We too shall accept the name for the time being. The Heavenly Slipper has a little light of its own, which is made immensely brighter by the light of the sun. Its present distance from the earth is around two billion miles. It takes nearly two years to revolve round the sun. Its size and weight is double of that of the moon. We were not aware of the existence of such an enormous asteroid before. We assume that it has suddely come into existence as a result of a group of asteroids suddenly knocking against each other. It has been knocked off its usual course due to the same reason. Its warmth and light is the direct result of the same cause. The sudden appearenace of this huge asteroid, has brought about some significant changes in the course of the moon and the Mars. Changes in the spring tide and neap tide have also occured because of it. Its present distance from the earth does not appear to be particularly dangerous but we strongly suspect that the planet in question is coming closer and closer to ours. We shudder to imagine what might happen if it actually comes too near!"

Several people were panic striken when they read this report. Some pot-bellied millionaires had heart attacks and kicked the bucket. Several more were suddenly striken by diarrhoea, giddiness, palpitations and asthma. Swamijis, mullas and priests had a field day, each preaching morality according to his religion. The literary stalwarts stopped writing fiction and poetry and took to writing about life hereafter. But the masses appeared to be unaffected by the panic. On the contrary, the discussion of the Heavenly Slipper led to jovial gatherings in every locality. The share-markets flourished as usual and the cinema halls continued to remain packed like before. But only for a while! Before long the reports which kept pouring in from the various astronomical centres froze the blood of the people. According to these reports the Heavenly Slipper was fast descending towards the earth. It was also beginning to clash with the earth's gravity, as was inevitable. In fact, a tremendous tussle seemed to be going on between the moon, the earth and the Heavenly Slipper. Calculations plainly showed that the last was bound to knock against the moon in exactly five month's time and then both planets were likely to crash down upon the earth. The resulting explosion would put a million hydrogen bombs to shame! The atmosphere was going to be totally annihilated just before the final crash came. The seas would swell up, covering the earth and every living creature would die of suffocation. There was nothing that anyone could do about it - except wait for the final blow.

All Christian communities brought out a joint petition which said - "Of course there is a great deal which all of us can and ought to do! Our elders were fond of quoting a couplet-

"If cold air reach you through a hole -

Go, make your will and mend your soul!"

But the Heavenly Slipper is no cold air blowing through a hole! It is the Final Judgement of God, come down upon us. We are bound to perish for the sins of mankind. Making a will is of no use. But we must mend our souls! And that, before we die! So, confess all your sins and clear your hearts. Pray continuously for God's mercy. Forgive all your enemies. Try to live for others and make others happy, so long as you are alive."

The Muslim, Jew and Buddhist religious leaders also advised more or less the same thing. Sri Byom Shankar Maharaj, distantly related to the great-great-great-nephew of Sri Adi Sankara, brought out a pamphlet in Hindi and distributed fifty millions copies of the same. What he said in the pamphlet was, in brief, as follows :

"Oh my children, my dear little ones, do not be afraid of death! I have already crossed ninety. Most of you are far younger than I am! But that makes no difference! The cares of the world are equally painful for the old and the young. All our souls are going to be released from the cages of our body before long. We are going to be one with the Divine. What is so scary about that? On the contrary, it is something to be wildly thrilled about. But we cannot discard our bodies while we are still unclean. That will take us straight to hell! Probably you all know that a patient is not allowed to eat or drink anything for quite sometime before a major operation. His bowels, kidneys, intestines are all cleaned out before the doctor performs the operation. The reason for this precaution? The fear of sepsis, of course! Now, just try to think how much more serious death must be compared to a mere hernia or prostrate operation! If the slightest impurity remains within our heart at the time of death, our soul is bound to turn septic. In other words, if you die without confessing your sins, you are bound to land up in hell! So, do not waste any time. Shed all inhibitions and false modesty and go, confess your sins. Every one of them! This confession will purge you and make you absolutely pure. But it won't do to whisper your sins. You must either shout them from the housetops or have them published in the form of a pamphlet, like I have done. In this pamphlet I have added a special postscript at the end, giving a complete and comprehensive list of all the sins I have committed so far. I have said quite frankly just how many bugs I have killed, how often I have secretly feasted on chicken, how many times I have lied and how frequently I've cast amourous and lewd glances towards my female devotees. You too should not waste any time. Start confessing your sins from this very instant."

In England large groups of men and women went on sin-confessing sprees, enthusiastically led by the scholars of Oxford. Other western countries also followed suit. The Indians, being more bashful than their western counterparts, did not pay any heed to Shankarji's advise at first. But they too were shaken by the fresh reports which came in from Paloma. According to these reports, the Heavenly slipper had come even closer to the earth, thereby weakening the gravity of our planet quite considerably. As a result, the inhabitants of the earth were already beginning to feel light-headed and giddy. The Doomsday was about be arrive - really and truly!

Men and women streamed out in large numbers and made a bee line for the nearest monument or park within the city. Then they shouted out the various sins committed by them. Another big group came out from Barabazaar accompanied by a loud band. They crossed Netaji Subhash Road and went right round the city. Hundreds of famous personalities joined them - all confessing their sins in soft, pathetic voices, beating their chests at the same time to give their act a greater impact. But the blare and din of the band drowned their words and nobody could make out what exactly they were confessing !

The B. B. C. played "Nearer my God to Thee" non stop. Delhi Akashvani played "Raghupati Raghava Raja Ram" while Radio Lucknow and radio Patna took to chanting "Ram naam satya hai" all hours of the day and night. Radio Calcutta echoed the strains of Tagore's "Samukhe shanti parabar". Radio Moscow alone remained significantly silent as they don't have much to do with the Divine! But our own President eventually arranged for a community "Pindadaan" at Gaya for the salvation of the communist folk at the

U.S.S.R, at the request of some of their own diplomats.

The four Big Powers - the U.S.A., U.K., U.S.S.R. and France - brought out "White Books" giving a complete list of all sins committed by them in the last fifty years. They also composed a joint slogan which proclaimed :

"Human beings are brothers all

There's no conflict - none at all!

The leaders of Pakistan said :

"Hindi, Paki - brothers true

But we must have Kashmir too!"

Amidst all these worldwide movements there was just one person who seemed totally unconcerned about it all. She was Bhuvaneswari Devi of Hatkhola. Strong and formidable in spite of having turned eighty, she had just returned from her visit to Kedar and Badri. She possessed an enormous amount of wealth and was totally free from the botheration of having to look after a husband and children. All she had was a pack of worthless dependants - all of whom she kept firmly under he thumb. Bhuvaneshwari was a devout dame - having learnt the Gita, Gitanjali and the Gita-Govindam by heart. But she had the reputation of being an atheist because she refused to be ruffled by gossip. Her panic-striken parasites surrounded her, frantic with worry, and said, "Madam Boss, the Heavenly Slipper is nearly here and the world is about to end. A huge meeting is being organised at the Jagannath Ghat where everyone is confessing his sins. You'd better do the same. Once you've got it off your chest, you will at least die in peace.

Bhuvaneswari knit her eyebrows savagely and said "what if I have sinned, eh? That is my business! Why on earth should I shout them from the housetop, you blasted idiots? This business of your Heavenly Slipper is absolute rot! There are millions of stars in the sky. What difference does it make if a fresh one appears? It's down right cheek to presume that the world is coming to an end just because you fools say so! I have several more years to live so you need not turn on the waterworks, any of you! what is God for? Haven't you heard what Tagore says - "My love would have been futile and meaningless if you had not been there to accept it!" What on earth is God going to do with Himself if He wipes off the entire universe and the entire human race? To whom will He show his miracles and how will He entertain Himself? Don't be put off by all this utter rubbish. Go and sleep instead!"

One can never explain why things happen the way they do. Possibly the Creator felt rather ashamed after hearing Bhuwaneshwari's words. Or perhaps events took that particular turn on account of the usual cause and effects of Nature's own laws. The long and short of it was that one fine morning all newspapers carried huge, three-inch-wide headlines which said "All danger is past. The evil star is about to disappear for good. All famous astrologers and astronomers have unanimously declared that the Heavenly Slipper is being pulled backwards pretty fast and is about to rejoin its old route. The mighty tug caused by Jupiter, Saturn, Uranus and Neptune is bringing back all asteroids into a single line. Which means, our earth has managed to have a narrow escape!"

The common man heaved a sigh of relief at this miraculous escape from disaster. But the uncommon ones were highly jittery. A big group representing all the big shots (in varied walks of life) within the country trooped off to Delhi and sought interviews with the Prime Minister. "Honoured Sir, we have confessed to all kinds of misdeeds in the last few days" they told him anxiously, "How on earth are we to manage things now?" The P.M. sought the advise of the Chief Justice of the Supreme Court. His verdict was as follows : "When a person confesses to a deed under pressure of police torture, the court does not accept the confession as legal. Similarly, confessions made under the panic of the Heavenly Slipper does not also have any legal value. Specially because no one had put it down in the form of an affidavit on proper stamped paper!"

The Big Four plus all the big and small nations belonging to the U.N.O. signed a protocol which said - "Everything stated as a result of the chaotic state of mind caused by the Heavenly Slipper is hereby declared null and void. Everything shall continue to remain just what they were before the appearance of the Heavenly Slipper."

The Heavenly Slipper has vanished from the scene once again. But it has managed to strike quite a few blows before its disappearance. We have lost a great deal of prestige. We can no longer hold our heads up and look people in the eyes because we confessed all our blunders.

The Exchange

I suppose you all know the actual story of Kalidasa's 'Meghadootam'. I'd better refresh your memories lest it has slipped out of your minds. A certain Yaksha who was one of Kuvera's assistants, tended to play truant once too often. So Kuvera cursed him and banished him for a whole year. The Yaksha set up a hermitage at Ramgiri and lived out his lonely existance. On the first day of "Ashada" the Yaksha discovered a cloud on the sky above. A cloud which resembled a dancing elephant. The Yaksha filled his hands with fresh bloomed Kurchi flowers and offered them to the cloud. Then he composed a long address in the *Mandakranta* metre and read it out to him. The gist of the address was as follows :

"Dear Cloud," said the Yaksha "I'm afraid you must make a trip to Alakapuri. Of course there's no mighty hurry. In case you get slightly delayed in order to have a good time on your way, it won't really make much difference. My languishing wife, your sister-in-law, lives at Alaka. Please relieve her mind by assuring her that I'm doing well physically but that my heart is sadly droopy because I've been missing her so much! The moment Lord Narayana rises from his eternal sleep, which means the month of Kartik, the curse inflicted on me shall end. We shall be united to each other soon after."

Kalidasa had not disclosed the name of that particular Yaksha. Nor did he tell us whether the Yaksha actually managed to return safe and sound after the period of curse. The Udyoga Parva of the Mahabharata mentions an exiled Yaksha named Sthunakarna. There's absolutely no doubt that this character was the same as Kalidasa's Yaksha, mentioned in his Meghadootam. Kalidasa did not write the actual conclusion of his poetic drama. He left it unsaid. Mahabharata also does not give us the actual history of the Yaksha. So here is the strange mystery which neither Kalidasa nor Vyasadeva bothered to spell out.

Not knowing the actual name of the Yaksha's wife, we shall refer to her as "Yakshini". Now, the Yakshini had been leading an utterly miserable life in her husband's absence. She placed a flower on a stone platform every single day. She would count them quite often in order to see exactly how many more would be needed to make up the required 365! At last a whole year ended. The month of Kartik came and went. But there was no trace of the Yaksha. Eager and anxious, the Yakshini waited for a few more days. Then she could bear it no longer. She went to Kuvera and fell at his feat.

Kuvera said "who on earth are you? I can see that you are extremely beautiful but why is your hair so dry and dishevelled? And your clothes so crushed and dusty? And why have you made just one plait?"

Yakshini burst into tears and said - "Your Majesty, I am the miserable wife of that ill-fated servant of yours whom you had banished for a whole year. His period of exile was over ten days ago and yet he has not returned to me."

Kuvera said, - "Why are you so upset? Try to be

a little patient. I'm sure he will come back eventually. Perhaps he has been detained somewhere. He is a young man, after all, and has been seeing nothing but flat-nosed Yakshinis and Kinnaris all his life. For all you know, he may have come across a beautiful woman there and has fallen flat for her. But don't let that worry you. He is bound to return once he gets tired of her."

Yakshini shook her head vehemently and cried - "oh no, no! My husband is not that kind at all! He won't even look at another woman. A cloud turned up at my place only the other day and gave me a message of ardent love and longing sent by my husband. My Lord, please be kind enough to make enquiries about him. I'm sure he must be in some danger. Or perhaps the tigers and lions have killed him."

Kuvera said - "I can't think why you are so put out! You are not likely to remain alone even if your husband fails to turn up. In fact, you can be mine and I shall see to it that you are very happy.'

"Please don't talk like that!" cried Yakshini horrified, 'Why my Lord, you are just like a father to me! My husband was exiled at your command and now that his period of punishment is up, it is your duty to see that he comes back. Rescue him if he is in any danger and if he is dead, let me at least know it for certain, so that I too can jump into my own funeral pyre and meet him in heaven."

Embarassed and annoyed, Kuvera said, 'You are a real pest! Very well, I shall go and look for your husband right now. I'd rather like to see Ramgiri myself. You'd better come along with me. Here, attendents, tell them to get my chariot ready, will you? Two of you must accompany us on the way."

The Yaksha had built his cottage on the top of a tiny

hillock at Ramgiri. Kuvera landed up there with his party. The cottage was quite a pretty one with proper doors and windows. But they were tightly shut. Kuvera asked one of his attendants to knock hard. "Hi Sthunakarna! Come on, out!" cried the attendant. 'His majesty, the great Kuvera has come to you himself. Your wife is here too!'

But there was no reply. Kuvera said -"There doesn't seem to be anyone about. So we might as well set the cottage on fire."

Yakshini said, "Don't you think of doing such a crazy thing, your majestry! I'm quite sure that my husband is here. I can smell fried fish. I'm sure he is busy cooking. The poor dear doesn't have a soul to help him here. I'd better call him myself. "Listen there! Do you hear me? I have come to you. His majesty is also here. Leave your cooking and come out. Quick!"

A window opened slightly. A female voice said - "Are you really here, Darling? And is His Majesty also here? What a catastrophe! How am I to appear before him?"

Kuvera was astonished. "Who on earth are you?" he cried, "You'd better come out fast or I'll set your house on fire!"

The door opened and a veiled woman stepped out of the house. Kuvera gave an angry snort and said - "Don't you dare put on airs! Take off that veil immediately."

The veiled figure bent very low and said - "My Lord, I don't know how to show you my face."

"Why not? Have you burnt it or what? Oh well, don't worry. You'd better smear some fresh dung from Lord Shiva's bull and your face will be healed instantly."

Yakshini came forward and pulled off the veil. The woman slapped her own forhead and cried - "Oh dear, dear! why didn't I die! Even death would have been better than this."

Kuvera looked at her and asked - 'Who the deuce are you? What has happened to Sthunakarna? Are you his mistress by any chance?'

"No, your majesty. I am your most unfortunate servant Sthunakarna. A divine curse has reduced me to this plight. But I assure you, the fault was not mine. And as for you, my love, we are the most unfortunate couple in the world! There's no way we can get united in spite of the curse having ended."

Yakshini said, "Your majesty, this person is really my husband. Look at his joined eye brows and the mole at the tip of his nose. Alas my darling, how did such a terrible thing happen to you? Which of the gods had you annoyed?"

Yaksha said, "It happened because I tried to help some one in trouble. There's no gratitude left in this world. Nor any truth either!"

Yakshini said, "But what made you turn into a woman?"

Kuvera said, "Oh well, such things do happen, you know, Ila, the wife of Budha, used to be a man before. He became a woman when he entered a private garden belonging to Parvati which was out of bounds for all men. King Riksharaja, the father of Bali and Sugriva, turned into a woman when he bathed in a certain lake. You'd better tell us your story, Sthunakarana, and tell us how it happened."

Yaksha started his story. "Your majesty, I had gone to the forest yonder nearly three months ago to collect some fuel when I saw a young woman sitting under a tree, crying her eyes out."

"Indeed!" said Yakshini 'What did the female look like, pray?"

"Not bad looking but not a patch on you, my love. A dry bony figure and not much grace about her! Well, your majesty, listen to the rest of the story. I asked her - 'Fair Maid, what's wrong with you? If you're in any mortal danger, I'll try my utmost to help you out."

Then she told me a strange story. She said - "Sir, I am Shikhandini, the daughter of Drupada, the king of Panchala. But my people know me as their prince Shikhandi. I was born as Amba, the eldest daughter of the king of Kashi, in my previous incarnation. Prince Bheeshma had taken myself and my two sisters away from the *Swayamvara - sabha* by force in order to get us married to his step-brother, Vichitrabirya. When Bheeshma realised that I was in love with King Shalva, he sent me to the latter. But Shalva told me - Look here, Princess, it is quite impossible for me to marry you. When Bheeshma dragged you away forcibly you must have felt thrilled by his touch. When Shalva said this to me I went and appealed to sage Parasurama, begging him to help me. He told Bheeshma that it was his duty to marry me and save me from this plight but Bheeshma refused point blank. Parasurama challenged him to a battle for my sake but even that failed to have the desired result. In fact Bheeshma ruined my life for good. I felt like killing him so I went in for a tough and gruelling meditation. At last Lord Shiva was moved by the earnestness of my meditation and granted me the desired boon. He said, " you will be born as the daughter of king Drupada. But you shall turn into a man later on and kill Bheeshma." Anyway, I was reborn as the daughter of Drupada. But I was brought up, like a prince. I can wield all weapons. In fact when I came of age, I was married off to the daughter of

Hiranyavarma who is the king of Dasharna. But the truth was soon out. My wife sent a message through one of her maids saying, 'Mother dear, you've both been cheated monstrously. The person you've married me to isn't a man at all. She is a woman!'

'When Hiranyavarma, my father-in-law, got to hear this, he was hopping mad! He sent a messanger to my father saying - 'you rascal! how dare you cheat me! I'm coming to see you soon with my entire regiment and four clever young women. They are going to examine your son. If they tell me that he is not a man, then I'll ruin your entire kingdom.

Finding my father in such a precarious and dangerous situation, I've run away from home. I've put all my dear ones in danger. I don't want to live any more. I shall stay here and fast unto death.'

"Your Majesty, I was filled with pity when I heard Shikhandini's pathetic tale. I told her, "Tell me what I can do for you. I belong to the court of Kuvera, who is the god of wealth. I can get the most precious objects for you" Shikhandini said - "Yaksha, please make me a man."

I said, "I can't quite do that but I could lend you my manhood for a few days so that you are able to save your father and his people from your father-in-law's wrath. But you must come and return me my manhood the moment your ordeal is over. My curse is about to end and I am dying to return to my wife. So come back the moment you're free.

Your majesty, Shikhandini ran away with my manhood that day and has never shown her face since. The wretched liar has maimed me by cooking up a cock-and-bull story and has shoved her useless womanhood on to me!"

On hearing Yaksha's strange story, the Yakshini cried out - "Upon my word, Darling, how could you be so crazy as to part with your invaluable masculinity just because of a few crocodile tears shed by an unknown female? Really you are an utter, and complete blockhead!"

Kuvera said - "Yes, you are nothing but a pig-headed donkey! Anyway, I'd better rescue your manhood . Come along with me!"

They landed up at Panchala in a body. Kuvera left his chariot in a lonely forest a little away from the capital and asked one of his attendents to take a message for Drupada's son Shikhandi. "Go and tell him that Kuvera, the god of wealth summons you instantly for a most important reason. Your entire kingdom is going to be reduced to shambles if you don't come at once."

Shikhandi rushed there pell mell on getting the message and touched Kuvera's feet saying, "Hail, king of Yakshas! Tell me what your command is."

Kuvera said, "Shikhandi, you have deceived my servant Sthunakarna badly. You have not kept your promise to him and have stopped him from being united to his beloved wife. If you don't wish to be utterly ruined, You'd better return his manhood double quick."

Shikhandi said - "Oh God of Wealth, of course I intended to keep my promise. I am sorry for taking so long over it. This noble Yaksha had done me a very great favour indeed. Do persuade him to lend his manhood for a few more days."

Kuvera said - "What on earth for? Isn't your ordeal over as yet?"

"Well yes, that particular ordeal is done with. The women who came with king Hiranyavarma examined me quite thoroughly and told my father-in-law that I am a real, through he-man ! On hearing this my father-in-law felt greatly ashamed of himself. He begged my father's pardon humbly, gave him a lot of handsome presents and returned to his own kingdom with his troop. He also scolded his daughter and called her a stupid a fool before leaving the place.

But even then, I beg Sthunakarna to grant me a month's time before I return his property to him. The battle at Kurukshetra is bound to end by then. I'll pay off my debt to Sthunakarna the moment I've killed Bheeshma,"

Kuvera said - "It's highly unlikely that you should kill a great warrior like Bheeshma. On the contrary, he is bound to kill you instead. And your manhood isn't going to be of any use once you are dead! So, nothing doing - and don't talk like a fool! Give back your manhood to Sthunakarna this instant and become a woman once more. If you don't, I shall go to your father-in-law with all my witnesses and tell him the whole story. Once he knows the truth he is bound to return to Panchala with his soldiers and wipe it out completely."

Shikhandi burst into tears and said - "oh dear, dear! What's going to happen to me?"

Kuvera said - 'I can't think why you should be so worried when your brother Dhristadyumna is there! Well, so are the five Pandavas and their friend, Lord Krishna. I'm sure they are perfectly capable of killing off Bheeshma between them!'

Shikhandi said - "oh no, that's just what they can't do. Bheeshma happens to be their great-great-grandfather and Dronacharya is their teacher. They can't possibly kill either of then. That is why I've been asked to kill Bheeshma and my brother has to kill Dronacharya."

But Kuvera refused to listen to any excuse. So

eventually Shikhandi was obliged to return the manhood of Sthunakarna and become a woman once again. An overjoyed Yaksha and Yakshini returned to Alakapuri with Kuvera.

An utterly depressed Shikhandi pondered over the happenings for a long long time. Then she came to see Lord Krishna. By sheer good luck the celestial sage Narada was also present there. Krishna said - "What's wrong, Shikhandi? Why do you look so exhausted? you were bubbling over with energy befitting a brave hero even a couple of days back! Why do you seem so soft and feminine all of a sudden?"

Shikhandi replied - "Basudeva, I'm in dire peril!"

Narada said - "well, you two had better have a tete-a-tete while I make myself scarce."

"Oh no, My Lord, there's absolutely no need for you to go' said Shikhandi, "you are well aware of my history. I've no secrets from you."

Shikhandi related all that had happened, adding - "Krishna! You happen to be a friend of the Pandavas as well as the Panchalas. My sister Krishna is a special friend of yours. Please save me from my predicament. I've been quite determined to kill Bheeshma since my previous birth. Lord Shiva Himself has granted that it shall be so. But how can I possibly fight until I get my manhood back somehow?"

Krishna said - "Your request is not quite a moral one. You have been born a woman. Why do you want to change into a man by a supernatural process? You'd better let somebody else kill Bheeshma. What do you say, Lord Narada?"

Narada said, "Really Shinkhandi, what Krishna says is perfectly valid. What does it matter if Shalva and Bheeshma have both refused to marry you? There is no dearth of men in this world! If you agree, I shall speak to your father about it and advise him to marry you off to a nice young man. He will make you perfectly happy and make a real woman of you. Your wife's misery will also come to an end. She too can marry your husband and you both can co-exist happily as cowives."

Shikhandi said, "Please don't say such things, My Lord! The boon granted by Lord Shiva is bound to come true. Krishna, there's absolutely nothing which you can't do. Please turn me into a man."

Krishna said - "I refuse to do anything so uncalled for! You can turn into a man only if someone exchanges his manhood with you voluntarily, like that Yaksha had done. But I don't think any one else is likely to be such a fool! Lord Narada, you keep moving around the entire universe. Can you think of a likely person?"

Narada said - "well, as a matter of fact, I can. You too know him quite well. Listen to me, Shikhandi. Krishna has a distant uncle at Vrindavan. His name is Ayan Ghosh - a 'Gopa' by caste. He is an extremely good natured, philanthropic man. But he is in a rather melancholy state of mind at the moment. He is totally indifferent to family life and spends all his time in prayers. You'd better go and seek his help."

Shikhandi said - "Vasudeva, please write me a strong letter of recommendation and address it to Sri Ayan. I can then take it to him."

Krishna said - "Have you gone nuts? He will throw you out unceremoniosuly the moment you mention my name! Now, look here, Shikhandi, I am rather ill-fated. There are some people who just can't stand me - although there's no rhyme or reason for their antipathy. Kamsa, Shishupala and respected Uncle Ayan top the list of such people. As a matter of fact, even Duryodhana, who happens to be the father-in-law of my son

Shamba, has turned into my enemy."

"What do I do, then?" asked Shinkhandi. Narada said "You should know what to do! You are familiar with all the feminine charms with which women capativate men and you are equally familiar with the diplomacy used by menfolk. In fact, both these are second nature to you and you can jolly well put them to use! come along with me and I shall introduce you to Sri Ayan.'

Ayan Ghosh lived all by himself in a little cottage on the bank of the river Yamuna, far away from the hustle and bustle of Vrindavana proper. He sat by the river one evening reciting the "Shiva-tandava - stotra" composed by Ravana, when Narada landed up there, Shikhandi in tow. Ayan bowed low and touched his feet respectfully, saying, "I' m overwhelmed by your visit, my Lord! But who is this beautiful maiden? I don't seem to know her!"

Narada said - 'She is Shikhandini, the daughter of king Drupada of Panchala. Lord Shiva has entrusted her with a rather touchy mission . She must remain unwed until it is successfully performed. But she cannot get on with her task without the help of some kind hearted and religious-minded man. Noble Ayan, I can plainly see in my mind's eyes that you are that fortunate man who can come to her rescue. Please honour her request. This paragon of virtue and beauty is going to marry you the moment her sacred mission is completed and make you the proudest and happiest man alive!'

Ayan heaved a long sigh and said I don't see much hope of my ever being happy again! In spite of being a married man I've no family to speak of. My house is empty. People despise me. They call me a coward and a fool and jeer at me behind my back. That is why I've run away from human society and have set up my cottate at this lonely spot. Why has this exquisitely beautiful princess turned to such a miserable object like myself for help?"

Shikhandi spoke in a honeyed voice and said - "Noble Ayan, the best-of Gopas, I had fallen in love with you even before I saw you, when I heard about all your virtues. I'm totally swept off my feet after seeing you in reality. I offer you my heart and soul. The whole of myself, in fact!"

Ayan said - "I had not imagined such a wonderful thing happening to this poor, ill-fated me - even in my wildest of dreams! My irresistible Shikhandini, there's absolutely nothing which I cannot do for your sake! Tell me what you want from me."

Shikhandi said - "Lord Narada you'd better explain it all to him."

So Narada told him the gist of the matter and added 'Noble Ayan, since Lord Shiva Himself has granted her this boon, Shikhandini is bound to succeed in her mission. You have to lend her your manhood for just a month. The battle at Kurukshetra is bound to end by then with Bheeshma safe in heaven. King Drupada will give you his daughter in marriage immediately afterwards. He will also give you half his kingdom and a good many cows and calves as dowry. You can forget all about your unhappy experiences at Vrindavan and start a new and happy life with your new wife in an unknown land."

Ayan thought for a while. But his doubts were soon cleared. He fell in with the request of his future bride quite readily. Shikhandi became a man once more and left the place with Narada with a light and joyous heart. Ayan-now turned into a woman - shut the door of her cottage to the rays of the sun and waited indoors patiently and eagerly for Shikhandini's return.

Bheeshma, covered with Shikhandi's arrows, lay on his arrow-bed on the tenth day of the battle at Kurukshetra. The battle finally ended after eight more days. But Shikhandi never come to Ayan again. There was no way by which she could keep her promise. Because Ashwathama stole into the tent of the Pandavas late one night and went in for a killing spree. Shikhandi was one of the murdered ones.

Poor Ayan was not destined to enjoy Drupada's Kingdom or have a princess for his bride. His manhood was also destroyed with Shikhandi's death. But we can't really say that his life went in vain. With time, Ayan underwent a wonderful religious transformation. He gave his heart and soul to Lord Krishna and came to be known as 'Ayani'. She learnt to play the 'Sri-Khol,' turned leader of the sixteen thousand Gopini maids who lived in Vrindavan and spent the rest of her days singing hymns to the glory of Lord Krishna.

Queen Buffalo

Hanseswar Ray happens to be a whacking rich man. The fact that his zamindari at Radhanathpur has been taken over by the Government hasn't made any difference to him, money-wise. He is the owner of sixteen large mansions in Calcutta, all of them located in office areas and other posh localities. The income yielded from these is well over twenty five thousand rupees. Moreover, he owns a large number of shares as well as a pawning business. Hanseswar is fifty. His wife Hemangini is somewhat indifferent to household affairs. She spends most of her time rolling in bed and tending her enormously bulky body with medicines and good food. She also reads a good many novels and scolds the other household members periodically by calling them a set of lazy louts. Chakori, their only child, has just acquired her Master's degree.

Hanseswar does not like living in Calcutta. It is not a suitable place to pursue his hobbies. On the contrary, Radhanathpur is ideally suited to this purpose. So he prefers to stay there most of the time. He has a spacious garden here and also a great deal of cattle and poultry. His fruits, crops and vegetables - mangoes, jackfruits, pumpkins and gourds- as well as his ducks and hens often win prizes in the agricultural exhibitions.

He has recently purchased an extra special buffalo from Gujranwala in west Punjab by bribing a Pakistani friend quite heavily. He has named the buffalo 'Queenie'. Queenie has just had her first calf. Hanseswar has made up his mind to send her to the next West Bengal Cattle Show. Rai Saheb Mahim Banerjee of Taldighi is his most powerful rival, being the proud owner of a Multani buffalo. But Hanseswar is confident that this time it is his Queenie who will walk away with the laurels - winning the Governor's gold medal.

Chakori stayed with her uncle in Calcutta while studying in college. But now that her studies are complete she has returned to her parents in Radhanathpur, though, she still goes to Calcutta for short spells. Chakori is tall and skinny, dark, buck-teethed and has high cheek bones. It is totally impossible to call her a beauty, inspite of her heavy and wonderfully put on make-up ! Her jealous classmates are of opinion that she attracts admirers solely on account of her father's fabulous property. Otherwise, she has neither looks nor any talent to write home about !

Hemangini is not in the least bothered about her daughter's marriage. Nor, for that matter, is Hanseswar. He says that since his Chakori is a smart, practical girl with a lot of practical sense, there is absolutely no danger of her moving around with her eyes shut - the way fools do - and falling in love with a useless, good-for-nothing fellow ! Nor is there the least likelihood of her being taken in by outward glaze and smart talk. In any case, what's the tearing hurry ? It's the done thing these days for girls to get married at the ripe old age of thirty or thirty-five ! So Chakori can easily look around herself and get hold of a suitable groom !

Amongst all Chakori's suitors, Bansidhar happens to be the most obstinate one. He has just completed his Ph.D. and has managed to get a lecturer's post in a college in Tollygunj, teaching Botany and Zoology. His father Sasadhar Choudhury died about two years ago. He was a lawyer and looked after Hanseswar's Calcutta property. Bansidhar's maternal uncles also live in Radhanathpur. So he visits the place off and on. Having known Chakori from childhood, he has always addressed Hanseswar as "Uncle".

Bansidhar having just come to Radhanathpur to spend his autumn vacation, went to look up Chakori and said - "What's the point in waiting any longer ? You have completed your studies and I too have managed to get a job of sorts. Surely you can't have any further objection to our marriage ? If you agree, I shall speak to your father about it."

Chakori said - "Please don't imagine that it's as simple as all that. So far as I am concerned, I can tell you that I quite like you. You are a nice, quiet sort - although you have an outrageously old fashioned name. It's exactly the sort of name one expects a snake-charmer to have. But you must know that I am not the sort to fall head-over-ears in love with anyone. I don't mind marrying you, if you can get my father to agree. But my father is not at all as simple as he seems. He is bound to come out with a thousand and one objections. But if you are determined and have the guts to face him, you may try your luck."

Bansidhar went to Hanseswar the next morning and told him very politely that he had something important to speak to him about. Hanseswar, busy supervising the morning rituals of Queenie, curtly asked him to hang on. Then he called to Queenie's keeper and said -"Look here, Gopi Ram, rub her down properly. There should not be even a speck of mud on her coat. Hey, what's this ? Mosquito bites on her nose ? Didn't you spray D.D.T. in her cowshed like I told you to?

"I have, Sir, and in large quantities too", said Gopi Ram. "But this 'Didi' of yours is no good at all ! It has no effect on the mosquitoes. If you permit me, I could easily get some bagulas from my village."

"What on earth is a 'bagula' ?"

"Cranes, Sir. If I keep some in the cowshed, they will gobble up all the mosquitoes, flies, spiders and other insects. Then the buffalo and her calf can sleep in peace."

"But why should the cranes remain in the shed ? They'll fly off in no time!"

"Oh no, Sir. I won't let them. I'll clip their wings so that they can't fly. An uncle of mine will be coming from the village in fifteen days' time. I could ask him to bring the cranes along, if you say so. Four of them will cost around twenty rupees."

"Very well. You'd better write to him today" said Hanseswar.

After giving Gopi Ram some more advice about Queenie, Hanseswar took Bansidhar to his office-room. "Well Bansi, what's all this in aid of ?" he asked. Bansi hung down his head, rubbed his hands and finally said, "well, Uncle, I have cherished a dream in my heart for a long time. I have come to beg for your consent." "Indeed !" said Hanseswar. "I suppose that means you wish to marry Chakori, eh ?"

"Yes, Sir", said Bansidhar in a timid voice.

"Look here, Bansi, I believe in plain speaking", said Hanseswar, "You are not bad as a suitor. You are far better looking than Chakori. You are also fairly learned and so far as I know, have a good moral character. But your financial situation is quite hopeless. I know that you have an ancient ancestral house in Calcutta but it's chockful of people. Absolutely teeming with your brothers, sisters, mother, grandmother, nephews, nieces and what have you. Chakori can't possibly live amidst such a crowd. I doubt if she can stay there for more than a minute. And as for your income, how much are you getting at this job of yours ? Two hundred ? And you hope it will be two-fifty before long ? Are you crazy, young man ? You think you can maintain Chakori on such a meagre sum ? Are you aware that just her cosmetics - snow, cream, powder, foundation, lipstick, perfumes, soaps and all that stuff - cost me more than two hundred and fifty rupees per month ? In case you are suffering from an illusion that I shall make lavish presents of money to my daughter and son-in-law every month so that they may live comfortably - well just forget it ! I intend to do no such thing !"

Bansidhar said - "How does it matter if I am poor, Uncle ? After all, Chakori is your only child. If you give her the money to live a comfortable life, there's nothing unusual or unnatural about it. In any case, she is going to inherit all you have - isn't she ?"

"The question of inheritence is a far-off one ! I still hope to live for at least forty more years. I don't propose to part with even a paisa before that happens. So long as my daughter is unmarried, I don't mind her spending my money as lavishly as she likes. But once she is married, her husband must attend to all her needs. In any case, won't it hurt your self respect if I pay for your living ? No girl can respect a husband who is dependent on her own father ! Moreover, why on earth should I pick out a charity-boy for my son-in-law?"

"Don't I have any hopes at all, Uncle?"

"You need not lose hope. Try your best to increase your present income. If you can manage to earn more than two thousand a month, I shall withdraw my objections."

"But I see no prospect of earning so much ! And is Chakori going to wait for me all that long ?"

"It's not for me to say how long she will wait. You can discuss it with her if you like. But you must know one more thing. If you bluff Chakori and marry her against my wishes, I shall give away my entire property to the Haringhata Dairy and invest whatever I have in improving the conditions of cattle and poultry. Besides, even if Chakori inherits my property, *you* are not likely to benefit from it ! She is an extremely shrewd girl and trusts nobody. She won't let you touch any of her cheque books or her money either ! At best, she may buy your cigarettes and give you a birthday gift each year. An expensive suit, or a wrist-watch or a Sharper-ninety pen ! I think you'd better give up your hope of marrying Chakori."

Bansidhar went away feeling really depressed. When Chakori heard all about it from him she said - "Well, I told you so ! I knew that father would come out with something like that."

Bansidhar said -"Chakori, your father is welcome to his property. I don't want any of it. If you really love me, can't you sacrifice it for my sake ? They say a woman can make any sacrifice for the sake of love ! If you love me, I am sure you can be happy even in my small house - inspite of my small income."

Chakori laughed outright and said - "Listen to me, Bansi. Love is a great thing, no doubt and I've quite a bit of it for you. But you know, love without money is just like a car without wheels - i.e., totally useless! Love evaporates if it has to battle with wants. And I am not the sort to remain content with just looking at your face amidst stark wilderness ! It's not in my nature. But

I am not quite the heartless demon father has made me out to be, either. I suppose he exaggerated a bit in order to get rid of you. I am not all that bad ! But I think father's objection is quite valid. I think you'd better give up your lecturership and try for a decent job. Father knows many of the ministers well. If you request him earnestly, I am quite sure he can manage a good post for you. The salary may not be very high to start with, but it may go up to two or three thousands later on."

"But are you going to wait for me all that long ?"

"I can't guarantee that. I don't believe in eternal love and all that rubbish. Both you and I may think quite differently in future. Now listen to me. Go to father and insist on his getting a good government job for you. But you'd better not go right now, because he is not in his right mind at the moment. He can think of nothing but his precious buffalo. His spy has just passed on the information that Taldighi-dweller Mahim Banerjee's multani buffalo is giving twenty seers of milk daily - which is a little more than what our Queenie does. Both are equally young and of equal good breed. So father is terribly upset. He has been feeding Queenie with crushed cotton seeds, groundnuts, spinach, peas, carrots, tomatoes, grated coconut, orange juice and what have you. He is also giving her B Complex shots. Let the cattle show be safely over. If Queenie manages to win the gold medal it will put father in an excellent frame of mind. You can ask him to manage the job for you then."

There was a full month for the West Bengal Cattle show to commence. But Hanseswar was off his head with worry. His Queenie had stopped eating and was giving very little milk. And it was all due to that wretched Gopi Ram, Queenie's chief attendant ! He had been boozing with his pals on the full moon night and created a big row. When the police turned up to knock sense into their heads, Gopi Ram cracked the former's skull instead. So naturally he was arrested and put in jail. When Hanseswar got the news he tried his level best to get him released. He even went to the extent of getting a good barrister from Calcutta for the purpose. The barrister pleaded that Gopi Ram might be released on an extra heavy bail. But his words had absolutely no effect on the magistrate. He sentenced the culprit to six month's imprisonment. Then the barrister said - "Your Honour, if this Gopi Ram is imprisoned it will bring about the total doom of Sri Hanseswar Ray. His Queenie, his champion buffalo, has stopped eating because she misses Gopi too much. And if she does not eat then how will she enter the competition at the Cattle-show ? So, your Honour, kindly accept a heavy fine and allow the culprit to take a month's leave. He shall return to the jail once again as soon as the Exhibition is safely over." But the magistrate was as obstinate as a mule and refused to listen to any pleas. So Gopi Ram was doomed to remain a prisoner until his term was up.

Hanseswar had no idea that his Queenie had grown so attached to Gopi Ram. He was off his head with worry. None of Gopi Ram's assitants ventured any where near Queenie for fear of being gored. She only allowed Hanseswar to come near her and stroke her back. But even he did not succeed in making her eat.

When Bansidhar got to hear of all this he came to see Hanseswar. He was standing with a bunch of Singapore bananas, trying to coax Queenie to take a bite. But Queenie resolutely turned her head away.

Bansidhar said - "Well Uncle, can I possible be of any help ?"

"If you want to be gored by her, you are welcome

to come forward" said Hanseswar in an angry voice.

Suddenly an idea struck Bansidhar. He moved away from Hanseswar and went to chat with Gopi Ram's assistants. He was able to collect quite a bit of information about Queenie. He took the early train the next morning and went to see Gopi Ram at the Burdwan jail. When the jailer learnt why he had come, he gladly allowed him to speak to Gopi Ram.

As soon as he returned to Radhanathpur Bansidhar went to Hanseswar and said - "Please don't worry, Uncle. I shall make your buffalo eat her food. I've learnt how."

"Indeed !" scoffed Hanseswar. "And may I hear just how you propose to do it ? She is going to gore you if you go anywhere near her !"

"It's not I who is going to feed her but you" said Bansidhar. "I've met Gopi Ram and learnt how he used to do it. It's perfectly simple, really. Whenever Gopi Ram fed Queenie he used to stroke her and sing a particular song. Queenie never touches her food until that song is sung."

"Its a strange state of affairs !"

"Well this is what the Russian scientist Pavlov calls conditioned reflex. Now, you'll just have to learn this song."

"Gracious ! I can't sing to save my life !" cried Hanseswar. "Anyway, what's this wonderful song supposed to be ?"

"But Uncle, I've a condition too which you must accept. You must promise me a generous reward if your buffalo eats properly - just as she used to, in fact."

"What is it you want, eh? Marrying Chakori?"

"We can discuss her later. If I succeed you must give me three of your mansions. That eight-storeyed one on Brabourne Road, the six-storeyed one on Chowringhee and the three-storeyed one on Southern Avenue."

"You really have some cheek, young fellow !" cried Hanseswar. "Are you aware how much those three houses fetch me every month ? Almost five thousands and a half !"

"Of course I know it" said Bansidhar. "But I can't settle for anything less, Uncle. You yourself have told me that you won't mind my marrying Chakori when I earn that much. Moreover, the advantage won't be all mine. You too will have to pay much less income tax and wealth tax every year if you hand those over to me."

"I never knew that you were such a blasted scoundrel ! Anyway, since there doesn't seem to be any other way out, I have to agree to your condition. If Queenie starts eating like before I'll give you the three houses. But if she doesnt, you are not to come anywhere near my house in future. See ?"

"Very well. I shall not."

"I've given you my word. Now let me hear the song."

"I feel rather shy about singing it. It's not quite the thing to sing in civilised circles. But since there is no way out, you must learn the song from me. It goes like this :

"Oh Queenie with her golden face
Has set my heart ablaze -
She has bewitched me, yes she has
And cast on me her spell !
Boompy boompy boom boom

"What a peculiar song!"

"Well Uncle, the song has a little history. Gopi Ram used to live in Darbhanga before he came here. A local nut used to sing this song whenever he passed the house of a certain Bengali family. But of course his version was slightly different. He used to say- "The Bengali lass with her golden face has turned my heart ablaze." Whenever anyone heared this song they drove the madman out of the street. Now Gopi Ram managed to pick up the song. He merely changed the "Bengali lass' to "Queenie". You'd better learn the tune and the words from me. There's no hurry. We can rehearse right upto ten O'clock at night."

Hanseswar did not like the idea at all. But he saw no way out. He tried his best to pick up the song with Bansidhar correcting him most painstakingly. "No, no, Uncle, not that way" he told Hanseswar over and over again. "You must pronounce the words just as Gopi Ram did. With his accent and typical Bihari twang. Otherwise it is of no use at all ! That's better. You are getting it at last. You just need to practise for an hour more for it to be perfect."

Hanseswar sent for Bansidhar early in the morning and said - "Look here, Bansi, you'd better come along with me when I go to feed Queenie and prompt me from the back. She is not likely to gore you if I'm there. One thing more. There won't be anyone else except the two of us. I can't possibly sing this song before any one else !"

"Very well, Uncle" said Bansi. "There is no need for anyone else to be there."

Bansidhar carried two buckets of food to the cowshed. Hanseswar poured it into Queenie's huge bowl. Bansidhar stood behind them and said -"Uncle, you'd better start the song right away." Hanseswar stroked Queenie's back and said,-"Now, now, my darling, please eat properly, won't you ? How will you put on weight and have adequate milk unless you eat ? That blasted Multani buffalo will defeat you otherwise. Come on, dear, come on -

"Oh Queenie with her golden face
Has set my heart ablaze -
She has bewitched me, yes she has
And cast on me her spell!"

Queenie heaved a huge sigh. Bansidhar whispered - "Dont stop, Uncle, keep on ! Keep on and on singing it with feeling and for goodness' sake, don't get the tune wrong !" Hanseswar kept to the proper tune and accent and sang the song thrice over. When he started the song for the fourth time, Queenie bent her head and put her mouth within the bowl. Soon came the sound of loud slurping and gulping of food. Queenie was eating at last!

The rest of the happenings need not be reported in details. Within a fortnight Queenie began to look like a Queen Elephant ! Her jet black complexion just glowed ! And she started giving twenty five seers of milk a day. She defeated the Multani buffalo and all others present at the West Bengal Cattle Show with the greatest of ease. The Lady Governor stroked her back. The Health and Agriculture minister carefully placed a garland of tuberoses round her neck. Queenie accepted it gracefully and stood chewing up her trophy !

When Bansidhar approached Hanseswar with his next request, the latter said - "What on earth do you need a job for ? You've grabbed all you could from me, havent you ?" Bansidhar said - "Well I shant have any self respect unless I hold a decent post as well. Otherwise everyone is going to jeer at me and say that I'm just making hay of my father-in-law's property !" *

---

*The central idea is based on an English story.

— author

The Letter Race

Sukanta Dutt is a real gem of a boy having acquired his Ph. D. soon after completing his master's degree. Now, having found a decent job in the fertilizer factory at Sindri he has been at it for nearly a whole year. Having lost both his parents early in life, Sukanta had been brought up by his uncle, whose letter he received just this morning.

He had written, "Sukanta, I've fixed up your wedding with Sunanda, the daughter of Bijay Ghosh who owns the Bijay Laxmi Cotton Mills. The family is a well known one. Moreover, Bijay Babu lives in Sankharipara and is virtually a neighbour of ours. The girl is quite charming and very fair. Although she was unable to get through her B.Sc. she appears to be intelligent. I am enclosing a photo of hers along with this letter. Since you belong to the modern age, you ought to have seen and selected the bride yourself. I can't imagine why you shoved on the responsibility on to my shoulders. Anyway, I have done my best and selected this girl for you. I hope my choice will meet with your approval. The wedding day has been fixed on the twenty third of Phalguna - exactly five weeks from today. Please make every effort to get at least fifteen days' leave. And you must turn up at least a couple of days before the wedding."

Sukanta read his uncle's letter very carefully. And also studied the photograph enclosed with the letter. Then he thought for a while and got out his paint box. Taking a piece of paper, he smeared three or four colours on it. Then he set it against his left wrist and tried to make it match with his own complexion. He thought carefully for a little more time and drafted the following letter·

"To Miss Sunanda Ghosh. Dear Madam, your wedding has been fixed with me. I have just come to know from my uncle's letter that you are very fair. But my own complexion is rather dark. You may have heard it but the word dark is a rather misleading term. It can stand for a variety of shades. I think it is my duty to let you know the exact shade of my complexion, so I am enclosing a piece of paper depicting the same. It's the exact shade of my left wrist. If you have no objection to having a husband as dark as I am, kindly drop me a line saying, 'no objection.' I am enclosing herewith a self-addressed envelop. In case you object, you need not bother to reply. If I do not hear from you wihtin five days, I shall understand that you are against this match. In that case I shall write to my uncle and tell him that I do not approve of this connection and that he should seek another bride for me. Yours Sincerely, Sukanta."

The reply arrived in four days time. "To Dr. Sukanta Dutta. Sir, I've no objection. But you are ignorant about the actual facts. In reality I am darker than you are. They had put on coats of paint my face when showing me to your uncle and the poor gentleman was fooled. But I do not want to cheat a truthful and honest man like yourself. I am sorry I do not have a paint box. I am cutting a strip from the sample sent by you and smearig a bit of blue-black ink on it to match my complexion.

No one minds a man being dark. But every one looks for a fair bride. Even the chap who is jet black himself wants to have an angelically fair and scholarly girl for a bride! So you need not feel any embarrassment on that score. If you object to my complexion please feel free to cancel the match. But in case you don't, then do drop me a line within five days. Yours Sincerely, Sunanda."

Sukanta sat down to reply to Sunanda's letter as soon as it arrived. " I don't mind your complexion being a shade darker than mine. But truth compels me to admit that I felt somewhat jittery at first. Because a beautiful wife is a real treasure, enhancing a husband's prestige and position. But I very soon realised that it was extremely foolish of me to think in these lines. It is quite obvious from your photograph that you are not lacking in charm, whatever your complexion might be. That should be quite enough. A dark complexion does not necessarily make a person ugly.

But I must let you know about a bad habit which I have. I smoke around fifteen to twenty cigarettes every day. I have heard one of my sisters-in-law remark that smoking causes a diagreeable charred stink in one's breath, which wives just hate but are too shy to say so. Of course it can't be true of those handful Bengali girls who have recently taken to smoking in imitation of British girls. But I am sure you don't belong to that class! If you object to my smoking, please drop me a line and I shall have the match cancelled. Sincerely, Sukanta."

Sunanda's reply came after four days. "I don't mind the charred breath. But I've heard that cigarettes cause cancer. Why dont you take to the hookah instead ? I don't mind the smell of hookah either ! I now feel that

I too should confess about a bad habit of mine. I chew nearly twenty to twenty-five paans each day along with tobacco ! So you can imagine how stained my teeth are! I've heard people say that those who chew too many betel-leves with tobacco smell of tobacco ammonia. My younger brother Lamboo has a nose more sensitive than that of a dog. He swears that he can smell ammonia whenever Krishna Sohagini Devi broadcasts her programmes over the radio. He can even smell garlic when one plays a record by Ustad Bade Gulam Ali Khan ! If you don't mind my paan-chewing, do drop me a line. Otherwise you may please cancel the match. Sincerely, Sunanda."

Sukanta's reply was as follows: "Since you don't mind my smoking, I am quite prepared to put up with your paan chewing ! Moreover we produce so much ammonia in our factory that I have got quite used to its pungency. I shall consider your proposal about the hookah.

I do not wish to cheat you in any way so I must confess about yet another fault of mine. Just as a husband wishes for a wife who has never known a man before, similarly a wife must also long for a husband who has never fallen in love before meeting her. I hereby admit that I do not possess an untouched heart. In short, I am not heart-whole. I had once fallen in love with Surangi, the daughter of commissioner Lala Topchand Jhopra. Her parents had no real objection to the match. It was Surangi who backed out at the eleventh hour. She has recently married Mr. Hanumanthaiya of the Commerce Department. He is jet black and looks like a *yamadoot*. But he draws a salary three times more than mine. The wound in my heart has nearly healed now. I am confident that it will disappear for good once we are married. I have a photograph of Surangi with me. I shall burn it in your presence.

After Surangi got married I realised that I too should get married without delay. I spend my spare time sketching, taking photographs and trying various scientific experiments. If I have a wife to take all house keeping worries off my shoulders, then I can pursue my hobbies with an easy mind. I have already realised that it is foolish to fall in love suddenly. The love that gradually grows as a result of a man and his wife living together is the real thing. One does not see an unborn child until he is born and yet his parents do not find it difficult to love him once he comes along. Similarly it hardly matters if a person does not see one's future bride beforehand. That is why I had left everything to my uncle.

Now I have told you everything about myself - my character, my temperament and my views. In case you approve of me, do drop me a line. Sincerely, Sukanta."

Here was Sunanda's reply - "I don't mind your character, temperament or views. It is quite obvious from your letters that you are a most truthful, honest and saintly man. So I too don't mind confessing my own weakness to you. I too had fallen in love with Pavan Kumar who was a post-gradute student. But he was a 'Bhaduri'- i.e, a Brahmin - so his old fashioned parents absolutely refused to have me for a daughter-in-law. Pavan is now in Bangalore, holding a very high post. I have not been able to forget him as yet but I am confident that I shall, once I get a magnanimous husband like you. In my opinion, there's no point burning the photographs of Pavan and Surangi. On the contrary, let's have the photos bound in a single frame and place it in our bedroom ! That might act as antidote to poison ! Don't you think it a good idea ? Please let me know what you think. Sincerely, Sunanda."

Sukanta wrote back - "Sunanda, I am addressing you by your name today because now there are no secrets between us. Nor any obstacles in our way. Folks tell me that I am a bit too serious. My uncle has also written that although you have failed in your B.Sc, you are an intelligent girl. It looks as though your temperment and mine are complimentary. According to psychologists, this is an ideal state of affairs. A match made to order, in fact ! It is the sixteenth of Phalguna today. Our wedding day is in seven day's time. I am enjoying the thrill of meeting you in person - in my imagination! Yours Ever, Sukanta."

Sunanda's final letter came a few days later - "I am in a terrible dilemma. Pavan Bhaduri has suddenly turned up. He came to see me yesterday and said - Look here, Sunanda, I am quite independant now. I also earn a decent salary. So, there's no need to listen to my parents any longer. You come along to Bangalore with me and we can have either a civil marriage or a Hindu one, whichever you want.

These are the circumstances. I expect you can realise my state of mind. I just cannot ask him to go away. In fact I am running away with Pavan exactly two days before your wedding. But I have my duty towards you too. I am not going away without providing for you. I have a sister named Nanda who is younger than I am. She looks exactly like me, except that unlike me, she is quite fair. She has also plucked in her B.Sc. But she has gleaming teeth and does not touch either betel leaves or tobacco. Nor has she ever fallen in love before. She has read every one of your letters and is fairly crazy about you. In fact she is dying to marry you. I beg of you, Dr.Sukanta, please don't make a to-do about this. And don't speak of it to a soul. Please turn up on the D-Day as per schedule, with all your relatives and friends. And do rattle off all the mantras dictated by the priest like a good boy. My father will do the giving away and marry you to Nanda. I am quite sure that she will make you happy. After all, you merely need a wife to take the house-keeping worries off your shoulders. So Nanda should do - just as well as Sunanda ! It's not in good taste to rave about one's own sister or I could have told you what a smasher Nanda is - in every way ! adieu for the present. If I get the chance to meet you later on, I shall beg your pardon in person. Sincerely, Sunanda."

Sukanta was bewildered by this letter. And also exceedingly angry. But being a rational and logical young man he soon realised that Sunanda's proposal was not a bad one. Since he was basically concerned with getting someone to look after his house, what difference did it make which girl he actually married ? Sukanta decided not to raise any hue-and-cry or try to make any enquiries. He would listen to all his uncle said and do exactly as he wished.

When Sukanta came to Calcutta no one at his uncle's place said anything about Sunanda. Nor did they seem the least bit worried about her doings. Sukanta turned up for the wedding with his entire retinue of relatives and friends as per schedule. But even there he saw no trace of any confusion. Sukanta saw a young boy of sixteen or seventeen serving paan and cigarettes to the guests. People there addressed him as "Lambu". Sukanta called him and asked - "Are you Sunanda's younger brother ?"

"Yes, I am" replied Lambu.

"What news ?"

"Fine. They are dressing up Didi right now. The ceremony is about to begin in a little while."

"Has Sunanda left already ?"

"What on earth do you mean ? Where can the bride possibly go ?"

"What about your other sister Nanda ?"

"You are funny! Don't you know that I have only one sister whom you will be marrying in a short while?"

"Indeed !" said Sukanta rolling his eyes.

Everyone had left the bridal chamber before midnight. Sukanta asked - "Who are you - Sunanda or Nanda?"

"Both. Sunanda is my proper name but everyone calls me Nanda."

"Why did you write such a pack of lies in your letter?"

"I had no evil motives, I assure you ! I was merely testing my truthful, magnanimous future husband ! I was curious to see how much you could stand."

"What happened to your Pavan Nandan Bhaduri?"

"Vanished into thin air ! He never existed. But I do have a nice picture of Hanumanji. We could frame it with your Surangi's photograph."

"You are an outright brat ! That's why you plucked in your exams."

"Oh well, in that case how could Jhuni Mitter top the class? She is much more of a brat than I am !"

"Really ?"

"I am quite hopeless in Maths. I can't understand Maxwell's theorem at all. That's why I bungled it."

"Why, that's a perfectly simple theorem ! Come, I'll explain it to you. Its just $V=$ root over ...."

"Stop, stop... it's terribly inauspecious to talk of Maths in the bridal chamber" said Sunanda.

"Very well, I'll explain it tomorrow then."

"Tomorrow is "Kalratri" and I'm not supposed to see you at all. We'll meet only the night after tomorrow at the "Phool shajya".

"O.K. I'll explain it the night after tomorrow then."

"Gracious! Didn't you know that it's a terrible sin to solve Maths problems on our 'Phool shajya' night? My grandmother is bound to eavesdrop in any case. If she comes to know that her grandson-in-law is teaching Maths to her granddaughter on the bridal night, she'll make you repent by forcing you to swallow cowdung! What's the mighty hurry anyway? I'm not running away, am I? Let a year go by. You can explain it to me after that."

"Just as you say. Let's go to sleep now in that case. You know, Sunanda, you really are beautiful" said Sukanta.

"Really ? Your vision seems to be pretty sharp !"

"Sunanda, do you know what I feel like doing ?"

"Eating me up, eh ?"

"Not quite. I wish I could - "

"Your wishes can wait. Just go to sleep now, will you ?"

The Truth Seeker

Vinayak Samanta has died in a hospital. In spite of being little-known, his had been an unique personality. He was as sincere a satyagrahi as Mahatma Gandhi himself. Except for one major difference. Gandhiji had the wisdom to come to a compromise when the situation really demanded it. But Vinayak was sadly lacking in that wisdom. Gandhiji had been assasinated by a half-crazy fanatic, either because the latter felt it necessary or because others had convinced him that it was the right thing to do. Vinayak died because he tried to fight the inertia and immorality of countless men - and that too, single handed. All of us are responsible for his death - in varying degrees. Circumstances often compel us to do the wrong thing. And sometimes we are compelled to put up with wrong doing in others. All this put together might be called the actual cause of Vinayak's death. He had no option but to die. Because there is no place for an uncompromising honest and unreasonable do-gooder in this world. Vinayak had failed to realise that it is just not possible to exist in this sinful world without making an occasional compromise with sin, however mild !

Everyone who knew Vinayak was convinced that he was not quite normal. "Crazy" might be too strong a term to describe his mental state. But eccentric he most certainly was. At the same time, every one was convinced that he was a totally honest man who loved his country most sincerely. He had joined the freedom fighters at a very young age. Later on he became engrossed in non cooperation and Swadeshi. He kept joining one political party after another. But after having been a part of the Congress, the Communist party, the Praja Socialist Party, the Hindu Mahasabha and others, he came to the sad conclusion that politics was a horribly complicated and sick institution and that one should break away from all groups and follow just TRUTH alone! One should go for the truth - be it pleasant or unpleasant - no matter what the consequences turned out to be. In short, he had taken to heart the two important teachings of the Gita - *Sarva dharman parityajya* and *ma phaleshu kadachana*.

I had not seen Vinayak for a very long time. He suddenly turned up one evening at our usual gathering, donning unusual clothes. He wore a light violet dhoti and kurta. A deep violet bag hung from his shoulder. I was quite astonished to see his attire.

"What's up, Vinayak?" I asked him, "Which party have you joined this time? I see a regular mob outside. Are they your followers, by any chance?"

"Shall I ask them to come in?" asked Vinayak, "There are ten of them. If all of them don't fit on this divan of yours, they can easily sit on the floor."

I gave my consent. Vinayak's companions came in, some sitting on the divan and the rest on the floor. Their age ranged from sixteen to thirty. All of them were dressed in violet and carried a violet bag. I was about to get tea for the whole lot when Vinayak stopped me. "We are against any kind of addications, - be it tea, cigarettes or paan" he said.

"Very good" I said approvingly, "Better relieve my curiosity then. I see you have made a new party. Tell me what it is called and what exactly your objectives are, in details."

"Ours is a group of Truth-Seekers. Our only objective is to propagate truth fearlessly. We intend to stand in this election."

"You don't say so!" I said in amazement, "How many do you have in this party of yours? Do you have the means to fight the election? How do you hope to contest against established parties like the Congress, the C.P.I.., the P.S.P. and the Hindu Mahasabha? And who on earth is going to vote for you, eh?"

"I didn't mean the general election" said Vinayak making a wry face, "And we are not asking people to vote for any one personally. We simply intend to make the voters aware so that they may not be duped by the words of scoundrels and vote for the wrong person."

"A good intention, no doubt. Why do you wear violet?"

"Violet is the symbol of truth."

"That's news to me" I said, "I always thought white to be the colour of truth."

"Oh, no. White isn't a proper colour at all. It is a mixture of all colours. You can verify it from a textbook of physics, if you like. I'll explain how it is. White is the colour of the Congress. Red is the colour of the Communists. The Hindu Mahasabha has saffron and the Buddhists and the Jains have yellow for their colour. Green is the colour of Muslim saints while blue is the colour of farmers and labourers. So the only colour which remains is violet. It is the colour of ultra violet rays. That is why we have chosen it. I shall now read out our manifesto to you. Please listen carefully."

Vinayak paused for a moment and started reading : "Oh my countrymen, male and female, young and old, rich and poor, educated and uneducated, all of you, BEWARE, BEWARE ! Whatever we are about to say is for your own good. We have nothing at stake, no selfish interest of any kind! You must, of course, excersise your franchise in this election. But don't you be duped by the smooth-talking cheats who ask you to vote for them. Find out, all about the candidate for whom you are about to vote, just as one tries to find out all about one's prospective son-in-law before one actually gives away one's daughter in marriage. As a matter of fact, this is even more important so you need to find out even more about the candidate you are voting for.

Don't let people convince you wrongly. Don't be taken in by high-flown speeches. Weigh each candidate carefully, judge for yourself who is the most suitable of all and only then must you vote for him. Don't, for a moment imagine that anyone belonging to such-and-such party - be it Congress, Communist, P.S.P. or the Hindu Maha Sabha - is bound to be good! And don't you believe that just because a person happens to be the leader of a party, he is bound to do good to his country and countrymen.

Don't vote for a dishonest, corrupt or an immoral man. Don't vote for a drunkard, drug-addict, opium-eater or a debauch. Don't vote for a liar and cheat who says that he is going to solve everybody's problems overnight. Or one who promises jobs to all and sundry, who promises to give homes to the homeless and double the income of the farmers and labourers. Or one who swears that the taxes are going to decrease and that food and clothes are going to be cheaper than ever before.

Don't vote for people who are thick with millionaires; people whose sons, sons-in-law, and nephews work in the offices of millionaires or candidates who are financed and maintained by millionaires. If any of them should come to beg for your vote, just throw them out unceremoniously.

Don't vote for people who brainwash little children and get them to canvass for them on the streets. Don't vote for people who have no minds of their own, who have sold their souls to a foreign power and are totally blind so far as that power is concerned, and who are unable to detect any faults in them. Don't for goodness' sake, pay any heed to what they say.

Don't vote for those one-eyed snobs who fix a salary for the poor school teachers which is lower than that of dock labourers, and yet don't mind paying three or four thousand rupees to the already rich officers. Don't vote for those who set up commissions and enquiries to investigate big crimes but hush up the findings. Don't vote for the wicked people who actually finance these rascals. Don't vote for those who adulterate our food, evade taxes and flourish on black marketing. Don't vote for those who make capital out of endangered Islam and endangered 'mother cow'.

"Stop, stop. You have made things amply clear" I said, interrupting him, "Yudhisthira himself, to speak nothing of Lord Krishna, is going to fail in this test of yours! Where on earth are you going to find the absolutely pure man who has never sinned in his life? You can't except people like Sukhdev Goswami, Gautam Buddha or Sri Chaitanya Mahaprabhu to make the budget of our country. Nor can you except them to run the milk business at Haringhata! If you need experts, you have to forget about their moral failings. If a drunken dabauch happens to be honest in the other things of life, and if the millionaires happen to be generous and given to charities and if a good speaker who is really concerned about the welfare of others is also a little dishonest about other things, there is no harm in voting for any of them! A moral, honest man who is both dumb and a nincompoop cannot possibly run the country successfully.

"Of course he can run it successfully" cried Vinayak, knocking on the divan excitedly. "No honest and moral person has ever had the chance to get into the Bidhan Sabha up till now so naturally he has not been able to prove himself! If only the people of our country turn a little alert and stop voting for the immoral, corrupt and sly fellows, then alone can really good people come to power and show the masses what they can do."

"Incidentally, how do you people manage to survive? " I asked curiously. "I remember you used to teach in the Ghughudanga High school at one time. Are you there still?"

"No. I was thrown out. I am now running a coaching class. These boys teach there too." said Vinayak. "Bhupesh, Jiten and Sailen here don't need to earn their livings because their fathers are all well to do people. Benoy here, teaches music to girls and Subal works in the firm of Badrinath Choudhury."

"Indeed!" I said amazed, "Don't you know that Badrinath had been arrested several times for selling adulterated ghee? He has had to bribe people through the nose in order to be released each and every time."

"Are you quite sure of this?" asked Vinayak.

"Of course I am. I happened to be his lawyer then."

"Look here, Subal, you must throw up your job today itself. I insist" said Vinayak.

"And what am I to live on, if I resign?" demanded Subal.

"A few days of fasting isn't going to kill you. Keep trying for another job."

I thought it about time to interrupt them. "Look, Vianyak, I quite see that your objective is a noble one. Now, what exactly do you want from us?"

"I want all of you to help us in every way. I shall leave our pamphlets with you. Please distribute them amongst people you come across. Give one to all your acqiaintances and explain our objectives to therm as clearly and lucidly as you can. And you must donate whatever you can to meet the expenses of our noble cause."

"I am very sorry" said my friend Hari charan, "We are small fry and cannot afford to fall out with the leaders! A fish cannot go against the sharks, alligators and whales while sharing the same water !"

"You are quite right" said Kali Charan, another friend of mine. "The safest policy is to remain neutral. How are we concerned about which the ruling party is? The Congress has made a tidy sum already. What does it matter if somebody else has a turn this time?"

Shiv Charan, another friend, also spoke up. "Listen to me, Vinayak. What you people are doing is tantamount to sedition!" he said, "It would be branded as 'waging war' during the British regime. We no longer have one king. We have a host of kings! Anyone and everyone elected to either the Lok sabha or the Vidhan sabha are our kings! We many vote for anyone we please because no one is ever going to find out who we've vote for. But we cannot displease anyone of them openly!" Vinayak looked directly at me. "What do you say, Brother? he asked.

I was bound to give a direct reply. "Listen to me, Vinayak," I told him, "All those whom you have met here this evening are good friends of mine. They are all honest in their own way, just as you are. Of course, I am not such an ardent champion of truth like you, but

I think I can be reasonably honest with you. All of us here are wordly people, bound to compromise with the ways of the world. For instance, take the case of Sri Sudhabindu Nandy. He is standing as a candidate for the Bidhan Sabha. The man is a notorious drunkard and a lecher, with two unsettled cases of alimony hanging against him. But he happens to be one of my biggest clients. If he gets to know that I have been helping your cause he will not give me a single case again! Then take the case of Mr. Radha Kanta Basu. He is a candidate for the Lok Sabha. He is a notorious thief and is known to take bribes left, right and centre! But my younger daughter is about to be married to his son. If I try to help your cause at this time such a wonderful proposal will come to naught!"

"What do you mean?" cried Vinayak. "Are you really going to mary off your daughter to the son of a corrupt thief, knowing full well that he is one?"

"Why not? It will make my daughter happy. Moreover there is no reason why my son-in-law should also be corrupt just because his father is! There is something more I have to say. My eldest son has somehow managed to get through his M.A. but is sitting idle and unemployed. And I don't approve of his comrades either! My friend Sri Girdhari Lal Pachari is trying to find him a cushy job. Sri Pachari is my friend, no doubt, but he is a number one black marketeer. What's more, he even smuggles rice, wheat, oil and cloth from Pakistan. Do you mean to say that I should ruin my son's future by annoying the man?"

"Does it mean that we cannot hope to get your support in any way?" asked Vinayak.

'Not quite, Vinayak" I said, "I, for one, have great sympathy for your noble cause. But you see how it is. The circumstances are too strong for me to be able to help you any other way. I can donate some money if you like but no one must know that I have given it."

'No thanks, we don't want any money at the moment." said Vinayak, "Good bye."

Vinayak returned to me in two week's time. His group was no longer such a big one. There were just three who came with him. "What news, Vinayak?" I asked him, "How are you getting on with your work?"

"The scriptures tell us that all good deeds meet with obstacles. It is very true." said Vianayak. "Seven people have broken away from our group!"

"Indeed? where have they gone?"

"Two have taken up ten-to-five office jobs and have no time to spare. Two others have taken up their studies seriously after a rude grilling from their respective fathers. That fellow, Benoy, who used to teach music, has suddenly fallen in love. So he does not have any spare time either. Of the remaining two, one has joined the party of your future in-law, Radha Kanta Basu and the other has been roped in by your friend-and-helper Mr. Pachari. Both are canassing for their bossses quite frantically, going about with loud speakers, screaming. "Vote for so-and-so". One of their henchmen came to threaten me recently."

"Really? Well, you seem to be in a bad fix, no doubt. Do you want some money," I asked him.

"Yes I do. But not as donation. I can only accept a loan. I might have accepted a donation from you if you had agreed to support our cause. I shall repay you as soon as I can."

"Very well. That should be good for your seif respect. But the corruption which you are fighting affects the entire country at large. What's more, it is being maintained by the big shots of the country. How on earth can you possibly fight them single-handed? You might lose your life in the hands of one of their goondas one day! So, for goodness' sake, give up this hopeless creed of yours! There are so many other noble causes which are not nearly so dangerous! Such as looking after destitutes, caring for the sick, educating the poor children, rescuing fallen women and the like. Please choose any one you like."

Vinayak was not one to be convinced. "Look Brother, everybody is not meant for every kind of work. I have chosen my mission in life and I intend to stick to it, even if I have to do it single-handed all the way. Do you remember how many opposed the British Government at first? Why did't they too choose a safe but noble cause? They died for their cause unhesitatingly and then other people took their place. Mine is a crusade too. I don't mind if I am the very first martyr. I am confident that there will be others even after I have gone. May be there will only be a few at first. But I am sure more will follow. Well, good bye for now."

After ten days a young boy came to see me. "Vinoo has asked me to give you this" he said, giving me a purse. "He has yet to repay you seven rupees and fifty paise. I shall do it on his behalf."

"Forget about repaying the rest" I told him, taking the purse, "How is Vinayak?"

"We admitted him to the hospital last night. I don't think there is the least hope of his surviving." said the boy. "He spoke to me at dawn and asked me to return you your money. Those were his last words. He has been in a coma ever since. He was very hard up and hardly ate anything at all for a whole month. He had become extremely weak. He fainted on the road last evening. That was when Radha Kanta Bose's car ran over him."

By the time I reached the hospital Vinayak was already dead. The three remaining members of his group stood there too.

Vinayak had returned all my money except for seven rupees and fifty paise. My help had been worth just that much to him. Supposing I had given him two or three thousand, would he have done anything else? What he really wanted was my active and sincere cooperation. Something I was not able to give him. Vinayak's mistake was that he had tried to destroy evil - something that only Godmen are supposed to do! Crazy Vinayak tried to do something completely beyond his ken and lost his life in consequence. The way an insect is demolished in a roaring fire. It is a great pity, no doubt. But this is what destiny is all about. There is nothing we can do about it. So we have no real reason to feel guilty!

The Transformation

King Yayati sent for his youngest son Puru and said, "Well my son, I've enjoyed your youth (which you gave away so willingly) for the last twenty-five years while you have been putting up with the heavy load of my age. I no longer care about the enjoyment of the senses. I now realise that enjoyment cannot possibly quench one's desires. It merely fans the flame of passion. Just as adding fat to the fire makes it all the more davastating! Hence the only thing one can do is to give up one's sensual desires for good. Although you are the youngest amongst my five sons, you are unquestionably the best of the lot. Your brothers are all selfish beasts who paid no heed to my earnest request. But you had given away your newly acquired youth the moment I asked for it and accepted my age, my falling hair, toothless mouth, wrinkled skin and failing senses. My son, you may please give back my age to me now and take back your lost youth along with my kingdom. Get married to a beautiful girl of your choice and enjoy all my wealth, living a long and happy, prosperous life. I shall leave my home and go and live in the forest now."

The story needs a little introduction. King Yayati's first wife Devyani, was the daughter of sage Shukracharya. She had two sons. His second wife

The Transformation

Sharmistha was the daughter of the Daitya king Vrishaparaba. She had three sons, of whom Puru was the youngest. Yayati had married Sharmistha secretly. When Devyani came to know about it she went off to her father's hemitage in a rage. Yayati lost his youth and turned into an old man all of a sudden as a result of sage Shukracharya's curse.

Puru listened politely to what his father had to say and replied - "Please forgive me, Father. I had obeyed your command once, but I've absolutely no wish to abide by this second command of yours. So please be kind enough to take it back. I have no desire to get back my lost youth. You are most welcome to go on enjoying it indefinitely. I am quite content with my old age."

Yayati said - "You astonish me, son! You had taken on my old age at my request. You're twenty-five years older now. I simply cannot imagine why you are not keen to shake your old age off you old age."

Paru said - "Just think of the present situation, Father. When you had taken away my youth and passed on your old age to me, I was just, twenty. You were sixty at the time. Twenty five years have gone by since then. You are now a middle-aged man of forty five while I am a grand old man of eighty-five. I am not in the least keen to acquire your middle age! Ever since I had old age inflicted on me I've spent all my time studying the scriptures, practising yoga and meditating about the Divine. Enjoyment of the senses means nothing to me. I've lost all desire for wealth and property. In any case, I happen to be unmarried, and even the most beautiful women cannot excite me. Nor do I have the least craving for the best of meat or sweets. I've no wish to give up this tranquil state of affairs. I am now busy meditating for my ultimate salvation. If I exchange my age with yours at this stage, all my efforts of the last twenty five years will go down the drains!"

Yayati, in spite of his middle age, looked no more than thirty with his raven black hair, moustaches and his strong and healthy physique. His eighty five-year-old son Puru had a head of snow white hair, a long and trailing white beard and moustaches. Middle aged Yayati was somewhat nervous as well as a little shy of his formidable old son. He said - "Well, son, I've certainly no wish to ruin your meditation of years but what am I to do? I cannot tolerate this youth-like and intoxicating middle-age any longer!"

Paru said - "The solution is a perfectly simple one. Give away your middle age to some worthy old Brahmin or Kshatriya and accept his old age instead. If you tell your ministers they will have your wishes proclaimed far and wide. I'm perfectly certain that there will be no dearth of candidates. You can exchange your age with the one you find the most worthy. Please allow me to leave now. I intend to perform a very special Yajna and have to make the necessary arrangements."

As soon as Puru left the palace, fifty queens of king Yayati left their inner chambers and rushed to him, surrounding him completely. His first Queen Devyani had left him in a rage years ago and had never returned from her father's hermitage. Sharmistha, the second Queen, was sixty now. She spent all her time indoors in prayers and refused to mix with anyone. When Yayati acquired a second lease of youth from his son, he took fifty more wives over the years. The age of these queens ranged from twenty five to forty. The seniormost amongst them spoke on behalf of the others. "What's all this hullaballoo in aid of, Husband? Is it really true that you are about to return your youth to Puru and take back your old age from him?"

"Yes, that's what I intend to do" said Yayati. "I

am quite tired of my youth and am keen to take up a life of meditation. But Puru is being rather obstinate about agreeing to my plan. He is no longer the dutiful son he used to be. He just refuses to surrender his old age as though it were something very precious. If I fail to make him change his mind I shall have to exchange my youth with some other Brahmin or Kshatriya who is aged."

Karanjakshi, the youngest amongst the queens, said - "Well, if this was your ultimate intention then why on earth did you marry us? you are the husband of several wives. You have enjoyed the youth of your son after your own. You may have got fed up of enjoying your youth but we have not! If you suddenly become an old man leaving us high and dry - it will be a grave sin on your part!"

Yayati said - "I've quite made up my mind and refuse to change my resolution. I release all of you from your existing wifehood. I shall also make you generous gifts of money. You can, all of you, get married a second time if you want to!"

"You're talking utter rubbish, Husband!" said Karanjakshi in a harsh voice. "All of us are mothers. Who, may I ask you, is going to marry any of us? A cow who has just had a calf may be doubly desirable but a woman who has had a child is no use as a prospective bride!"

"Oh very well, very well! I shall make some arrangement for you so that you may be able to live happily - even if you fail to get hold of a second husband" said Yayati in exasperation. "For goodness' sake, get lost now. I've a lot of things to do."

Yayati tried his level best to get his son to change his mind. But it was of no use. So the minister got busy making the following announcement: "All you learned and cultured old people from good Brahmin and Kshatriya families, listen to me carefully. King Yayati, the renowned Kuru king, does not wish to enjoy his youth any longer. He therefore wishes to exchange his youth with some worthy old man. Shri Yayati is forty five now, as fresh and glowing as a young man. All prospective candidates should assemble at the palace hall of Hastinapur next new moon, around midday. The king himself will select his candidate and exchange his youth with whoever he considers to be the most suitable. His decision will be final. No protests will be allowed."

Nearly a thousand Brahmins and Kshatriyas - bent with age - turned up at the Hastinapur palace on the day scheduled for the exchange. Their age ranged from sixty to a hundred. Some were hunch-backed and leaned on sticks. Some were totally blind and walked holding the hands of others. Some could not walk at all and had to be carried inside. Hearing of Yayati's announcement, the two Ashwini brothers from heaven and sage Narada also turned up at the palace, eager to watch the fun. But they came in disguise and no one could recognise them.

Yayati greeted all the candidates present and was about to examine them when a group of old women pushed through the crowd and stood before king Yayati. Their leader was an elderly Brahmin lady. Although there was hardly any hair on her head, she wore the big red vermillion dot on her forehead signifying her marital status and also a glowing red sari. Speaking in a trembling voice she addressed Yayati saying, -"According to the scriptures, youth, wealth, ownership and heedlessess are damaging traits. Each of these can bring about utter ruin. Unfortunately, you have all four at one and the same time. A single lifetime of youth is bad enough, but you have enjoyed two of them! So you can well imagine what an old man who has enjoyed two youths in one lifetime is going to be like! The moment you exchange this kind of youth with an old man, he will rush out to get hold of a young wife. Can you imagine what his old wife is going to do when this happens? Or what her feelings will be?"

Yayati looked ashamed and said - "You are quite right. Here, Minister, please anounce at once that I shall not exchange my youth with anyone who has wives living. Please offer them a gold coin on my behalf and request them to leave."

All those with wives accepted their coin but sat where they were - eager to see whom the king would select.

The old Brahmin who had been carried indoors asked his bearers to carry him before the king. Then he said - "Victory to you, my king. I am Kuliraka, a most learned man, well versed in every scirpture and am a hundred years old. I had five wives but they are all dead now. I am sure you will never find a more suitable candidate than myself. So please exchange your youth with me."

Yayati greeted him respectfully and said - "Noble Lord, I wish to accept age, no doubt, but I've no wish to become a cripple ! Minister, please give him five gold coins and get rid of him."

The next candidate was a hunch-backed old man who ambled up to Yayati holding the hands of his two grandsons. "Your majesty, I am Kinchuluka, a descendant of Karataviryarjuna. I am eighty. I am rather short of vision. People call me Pragya-Chakshu on account of my infinite knowledge and wisdom. But I am unhappy although I have a good many grandsons. Everyone ignores me, and longs for my death because they have their eyes on my property. If only I could have your mellow youth, I'd get married once again and be happy at long last."

Yayati replied -" Well, wise Kinchuluka, I do want to exchange my youth but your vision of wisdom is not going to be of any use to me. Minister give him five gold coins and send him packing."

Countless candidates faced Yayati, poetising on their special qualifications but Yayati did not consider any of them worthy of the great "exchange"! Suddenly there was a buzz among the masses as they respectfully made way for a couple of white-haired, white-bearded old men who held the hands of an exceedingly beautiful and charming damsel and walked up to the king.

Yayati stared at them in surprise and said - "who may you be, my Lords? And who is this non-pareil whose beauty has lit up my entire court with its dazzling glow ?"

The brother, who was obviously the older, replied - "Sir, we are from the Vilvashrama hermitage, situated at the foothills of the Vindhya range. You must be familar with the name of the great sage Bhallataka. I am his elder son Bibhitaka and this is my younger brother Haritaka. The exquisite damsel with us is Manohara, the daughter of Mitrasena, the king of Subarta.

When Mitrasena lost his wife, he decided to hand over his kingdom to his son and lead a life of meditation. Then he tried to find a suitable groom for his daughter. But Manohara who was the only daughter of the king, protested saying - " There's no need to get me married, Father! Do take me to the forest with you. Otherwise, who is gcing to look after you there?" Seeing her eagerness, the king relented. As our father, sage Bhallataka, was his ancestral Guru, he built his hut near his hermitage and started living there with his daughter. Our father, being fairly advanced in age, passed away after some time. King Mitrasena followed him after a fifteen-year-spell in the forest. He told us at the time of death - "Alas my time has come before I could get my daughter wedded! Brother Bibhitaka, Brother Haritaka, you two must look after her. Get her married immediately. But mind you, not with an old man. My daughter won't be able to stomach a superannuated spouse. "This put us in a tremendous quandry. We are both fairly aged and hence cannot be proper candidates for Manohara. We were just wondering what we should do when, we heard your announcement. That is why we rushed here Your majesty, I am worthy of Manohara in every way so please exchange your youth with me. Once I'm young, nothing can stand in the way of our marriage."

Haritaka, enraged and excited, cried - "Your Majesty, what my brother says is totally wrong and improper. I am a better scholar than he is and far more handsome. Moreover the gap between my age and that of Manohara is far less. She is thirty while I am sixty. My brother is sixty-five. Naturally I am far more suited to marry her than he is. All the more so, if you grant me your youth."

Bibhitaka blew his top at his brother's impertinance and cried - "Shut up, you fool! How can the younger brother possibly marry before the elder one ?"

Yayati looked at Manohara and asked - "What is your opinion, Princess? I shall give my youth to the one you suggest. Whom do you prefer between these two?"

Manohara said - "Both are the same to me."

Yayati said - "Well my Beautiful One, you have really put me in a quandry. Personally speaking, I too don't feel that there is anything to choose between these two. Now, I wonder if I could do something... Just look at me once, will you?"

Yayati stroked his raven black curly hair and twirled his regal mustache. Then he said - "I already have youth - a blazing, flaming youth! Suppose I were to retain it - and if I were to marry you myself, Manohara! How would you like it?"

Bibhitaka and Haritaka were absolutely furious and cried - "what do you mean by this outlandish behaviour, Your Majesty? You had proclaimed far and wide that you'd make a gift of your youth. How dare you sing a different tune now?"

The assembled oldies waved their hands vigourously and shouted - "Your Majesty, if you break a sacred promise, you shall burn in hell forever! What obnoxious cheek to send for us and then deceive us like this!"

The assembled masses took up the chant "wont do! Won't do!" in a feverish frenzy.

Finding matters speedily going out of hand, sage Narada and the two Ashwini Kumars made an appearance. Yayati tried to greet them with proper reverence but Narada stopped him saying "Don't put yourself out at the moment. Try to get over this crisis instead."

Yayati said - "Celestial Sage, my head feels dizzy! Kindly advise me as to what I should do."

Narada said - "Well, you have broken your word and strayed from the path of truth. You'd better send for Puru right away. He will arrange about your making amends."

Puru entered the packed hall on receiving the Royal summons. He greeted his elders respectfully and said - "What do you mean by involving me in all this, father? My Yajna is not yet complete and I haven't even had my final ritualistic bath. I had to rush here leaving everything incomplete because you sent for me. Now tell me, what do I have to do?"

Yayati stood silent. Narada told Puru - "Well prince, your father is suffering from a slight imbalance of the heart and it is up to you to put him straight. You must decide with whom he should exchange his youth from this assembled crowd of old men."

Puru looked around him and asked - "Who is that dazzling beauty whose hands are being held by two old men?"

Narada replied, "She is princess Manohara, daughter of the late king of Subarta. The two old men are the sons of his late Guru. They are Bibhitaka and Haritaka and both are suitors for Manohara's hand. As a matter of fact, both have come here to exchange their age with your father's youth. But your father is faced with a terrible problem because he is unable to decide with whom he should do it."

Puru said - "I don't see any problem at all. I'll solve the question in a jiffy. Princess, which of these two old men do you consider to be worthier?"

Manohara said - "There's absolutely nothing to choose between the two."

Puru thought a while and said - "Exquisite Manohara, I'd like to discuss the question with you in private. Come, let us decide it once for all in the shade of that Ashok tree over yonder."

After talking things over under the Ashok tree, Puru faced the assembled crowd and said - "My most respected Father, sage Narada, Revered Celestial surgeons Kumars Ashwini, Gentlemen at the court who have assembled today, lend me your ears. The realisation has suddenly dawned upon me that it was a grave failing on my part to have ignored and disobeyed my father's orders. I beg his pardon humbly here and now and request him to accept my age - as he wanted to do all along - and grant me his youth instead. Princess Manohara has promised to accept me as her husband."

"Bravo, bravo! " cried sage Narada and the two Ashwini Kumars.

"Long live king Yayati! Long live Puru, the Prince Regent!" Cried the assembled masses. Bibhitaka and Haritaka made a wry face and quietly made themselves scarce.

Yayati softly muttered to himself - 'Shame, shame, shame! What on earth induced you to say 'No' to my offer so arrogantly the other day, if this is what you meant to do? Why make such an exhibition before the public ?"

The two celestial surgeons said - "King Yayati, prince Puru, we'll perform the operation right now and exchange the youth of one with the age of the other. We have brought along all the necessary surgical instruments."

Sage Narada said - "You two won't have to do a thing. The transformation shall take place automatically and instantly."

Puru bent down and touched his father's feet. Yayati laid his hand on his son's head and said - "May you have my youth and I, your age."

In a moment the transformation was complete!